OLIVER TWIST

Charles Dickens

OLIVER TWIST

PETER HADDOCK PUBLISHING

Published in this edition 1997 by Peter Haddock Publishing,
United Kingdom
Reprinted 1999, 2004

© 1997 This arrangement, text and illustrations,
Geddes & Grosset, David Dale House,
New Lanark, Scotland

Illustrated by Andrew Geeson (Simon Girling Associates)

ISBN 0 7105 0934 0

Printed and bound in Poland

Contents

To the Reader

I am sure you will have seen a film, or watched a programme on TV, that has been made from some famous book. If you enjoyed the film or programme, you may have decided to read the book.

Then what happens? You get the book and, it's more than likely, you get a shock as well! You turn ten or twenty pages, and nothing seems to *happen*. Where are all the lively people and exciting incidents? When, you say, will the author get down to telling the story? In the end you will probably throw the book aside and give it up. Now, why is that?

Well, perhaps the author was writing for adults and not for children. Perhaps the book was written a long time ago, when people had more time for reading and liked nothing better than a book that would keep them entertained for weeks.

We think differently today. That's why I've taken some of these wonderful books, and retold them for you. If you enjoy them in this shorter form, then I hope that when you are older you will go back to the original books, and enjoy all the more the wonderful stories they have to tell.

About the Author

Charles Dickens was born at Portsmouth in 1812 and died at Gadshill in 1870. He suffered many hardships as a child. In 1824 his father was sent to prison for debt and Charles was left to earn his own living in a factory. These early experiences are reflected in his novels, most of which describe the terrible things that went on in the England of his day.

Chapter One
In the Workhouse

Oliver Twist was born in a workhouse; and on the day that he was born his poor young mother died.

"She was a good-looking girl," said the doctor, pausing by the bedside. "Where did she come from?"

But nobody knew.

"She was brought here last night," said the pauper woman who had acted as nurse. "She was found lying in the street."

The parish authorities sent him to a branch workhouse, three miles off—a baby farm, where an old woman named Mrs. Mann took charge of him, for sevenpence-halfpenny a week.

But despite the meagre food and scant clothing, Oliver lived to be nine years old; and he was spending his ninth birthday in the coal cellar with two other boys, who had been locked up there with him, after a sound thrashing from Mrs. Mann, because they had actually complained that they were hungry.

Mrs. Mann had just drawn the bolt of the cellar door when she was startled to see Mr. Bumble—the beadle of the workhouse where Oliver was born—trying to undo the latch of the garden gate.

"Goodness gracious! Is that you, Mr. Bumble, sir?" said Mrs. Mann, thrusting her head out of the window. And then she whispered to the girl who helped her, "Susan, take Oliver and them two other brats upstairs, and wash 'em directly. My heart alive! Mr. Bumble, how glad I am to see you, surely."

"I am sure, Mr. Bumble, I was only a-telling the dear children, as is so fond of you, that it was you a-coming," said Mrs. Mann.

"Well, well, Mrs. Mann," replied the beadle. Lead the way, Mrs. Mann, for I have come on business."

Mrs. Mann ushered him into a small parlour with a brick floor, and officiously put his cocked hat and cane on the table before him.

"Now," said Mr. Bumble, "The child that was baptized Oliver Twist is nine years old today. And notwithstanding an offered reward, we have never been able to discover who his father is, or what was his mother's name."

"How comes he to have any name at all, then?" asked Mrs. Mann.

The beadle drew himself up with great pride, and said, "I invented it."

"You, Mr. Bumble?"

"I, Mrs. Mann. We name our foundlings in reg'lar alphabet order. The last was S,—Swubble, I named him. This was a T,— Twist, I named *him*. The next one that comes will be Unwin, and the next Vilkins and so on."

"Why, you're quite a lit'rary character, sir!" said Mrs. Mann.

"Well, well," said the beadle, "perhaps I may be. Perhaps I may be, Mrs. Mann." He added that Oliver being now too old to remain at the baby farm, the managers had determined to have him back into the House. "I have come out myself to take him there," said Mr. Bumble.

Mr. Bumble took him away to the old workhouse where he was born, and into a large whitewashed room, where eight or ten fat gentlemen were sitting round a table.

They were the managers of the workhouse, and after having asked Oliver his name, they told him that as he had no father or mother or anybody belonging to him, he was to be educated there, and taught a useful trade.

Life at the workhouse was not any better than at Mrs. Mann's, and there was not much more to eat; one boy, indeed, got so ravenous at last that he hinted darkly to his companions that unless he had something more to eat he was afraid he would wake up so hungry some night that he would eat the boy that slept next him.

So a council was held, and lots were cast as to who should walk up to the master after supper that evening, and ask for more; and the lot fell on Oliver Twist.

The boys were fed in a large stone hall, with a large pot at the end in which the gruel was cooked. The evening arrived; and the boys took their places. The master took his station at the pot and ladled out the gruel into basins. Each boy was allowed one basin, and no more.

The boys swallowed it ravenously; it soon disappeared, and then they whispered and winked at Oliver.

Oliver rose from his seat. It was a bold thing to do; but he was desperate with hunger, and, advancing to the master with his basin in his hand, he said, trembling: "Please, sir, I want some more."

"What?" said the master.

"Please, sir, I want some more."

The master aimed a blow at Oliver's head with the ladle; then he held him by the arms, and shouted for the beadle.

Mr. Bumble came rushing in.

"Oliver Twist has asked for more!"

Then there was a tremendous fuss. Oliver was confined in a dark and solitary room, and the next morning a notice was hung on the outside of the gate, offering a reward of five pounds to anybody who would take him off the hands of the parish and apprentice him to a trade.

One morning a chimney sweep passed that way, and read the notice on the gate.

He owed five pounds to his landlord, and he fancied he saw a very easy way of paying it.

One of the managers—a fat gentleman in a white waistcoat—happened to be standing at the gate. "This here boy, sir," said the chimney sweep, addressing him, "wot the parish wants to 'prentice."

"What of him?" asked the gentleman in the white waistcoat.

"I am ready to take him!"

"Walk in," said the gentleman in the white waistcoat. And he took the chimney sweep into the room where the other managers were sitting.

"It's a nasty trade," said one gentleman, when he had heard what the chimney sweep wanted.

For in those days chimneys were not swept with long-handled brushes as they are swept now. Young boys climbed up the chimneys, scraping down the soot as they went.

"It's such a nasty business," put in another gentleman, "that you ought to take something less than the premium we offer."

So, after a good deal of bargaining on both sides, the chimney sweep agreed to take Oliver for three pounds ten shillings.

Then Oliver was summoned, and Mr. Bumble told him pompously that he was going to be made "a 'prentice of."

"A 'prentice, sir?" asked the poor little boy, trembling.

"Yes, Oliver," said the beadle. "The kind and blessed gentlemen, are going to 'prentice you, and to set you up in life, and make a man of you, although the expense to the parish is three pound ten!"

Mr. Bumble told him he was to appear before the magistrates,

and that if the gentlemen asked him if he wanted to be apprenticed he was to say, "Yes," immediately.

Oliver followed the beadle, with a beating heart, into a large room where two old gentlemen sat behind a desk.

One was reading a newspaper, and the other was looking at the agreement through a pair of tortoiseshell spectacles. One of the managers was standing in front of the desk, on one side; and the chimney sweep, with a dirty, evil-looking face, on the other.

After Oliver was introduced and had made his bow, the magistrate with the tortoiseshell spectacles said, "I suppose he's fond of chimney sweeping."

"He dotes on it, your worship," said Mr. Bumble, giving Oliver a sly pinch to intimate that he had better not say he did not.

Oliver was too frightened to speak. He was looking at the cruel face of his future master, and grew more frightened than ever.

"And this man that's to be his master—you, sir—you'll treat him well, and feed him, will you?" said the old gentleman.

"I will, indeed I will," said the chimneysweep doggedly.

The old gentleman took up his pen to sign the agreement, when his eyes suddenly encountered the terrified face of the poor little boy, looking at the chimney sweep with fear and horror.

He put down his pen, leaned over the desk, and stared at Oliver.

"My boy!" said the old gentleman, "you look pale and frightened. What is the matter?"

Oliver fell on his knees, and, clasping his hands together, prayed the magistrates to starve, or beat, or kill him, rather than send him away with that cruel-looking man.

Then the gentleman in the tortoiseshell spectacles nodded to the other magistrate, and, tossing aside the agreement on the desk, said, "We refuse to sign these papers."

And the other magistrate added sharply, "Take the boy back to the workhouse, and treat him kindly."

The next morning the notice was put up on the gate again.

Chapter Two
At Mr. Sowerberry's

The beadle was on his way home one day soon afterwards when he met at the gate Mr. Sowerberry, the undertaker.

"By-the-bye, you don't know anybody that wants a boy, do you?" asked Mr. Bumble. "Liberal terms, Mr. Sowerberry," and he pointed to the notice on the gate.

"Goodness!" said the undertaker. "That's the very thing I have been meaning to speak with you about; I think I should like to take the boy myself."

After a little talk with the managers, it was agreed that Oliver should be sent on trial to the undertaker's, as house-boy, that very evening.

Oliver took the news in silence; and with a shirt and a pair of socks tied up in a brown-paper parcel in his hand, he was led away by Mr. Bumble.

The undertaker had just put up the shutters of his shop, and was writing by the light of a dismal candle when the newcomers entered. And Mr. Bumble told Oliver to make a bow.

"Oh! that's the boy, is it?" said the undertaker, lifting the candle above his head to get a better view. "Mrs. Sowerberry, will you have the goodness to come here, my dear?"

A little thin woman appeared.

"My dear," said Mr. Sowerberry, "this is the boy from the workhouse that I told you of."

Oliver bowed again.

"Dear me," said Mrs. Sowerberry, "he's very small."

"Why, he *is* rather small," said Mr. Bumble, looking at Oliver as if it were Oliver's own fault that he was no bigger. "He *is* small. But he'll grow, Mrs. Sowerberry—he'll grow."

She took Oliver down a flight of dark stairs into a stone-floor kitchen, where a girl was sitting.

"Here, Charlotte," said Mrs. Sowerberry, "give this boy some of the cold bits that were put by for Trip. I daresay the boy isn't too dainty to eat them. Are you, boy?"

Oliver said, "No," eagerly. His eyes were glistening at the sight of meat; and he sat down before the plateful of coarse broken food that had been kept for the dog, and ate it ravenously.

Mrs. Sowerberry gazed at him in horror. "Well!" she exclaimed.

Come with me," said Mrs. Sowerberry, taking up a dim and dirty lamp, and leading the way upstairs. "Your bed is under the counter. You don't mind sleeping among the coffins, I suppose? But it don't much matter whether you do or you don't, for you can't sleep anywheres else."

Oliver meekly followed his new mistress. And there in the shop, under the counter, she showed him his bed, and left him to himself. Oliver put the lamp on a workman's bench, and gazed timidly round the shop. A half-finished coffin on black trestles stood in the middle, and on the wall hung a picture of a hearse.

Oliver felt very much alone and crept quietly to bed where he took a long time to get to sleep.

A loud kicking at the outside of the shop door awoke him next morning. He jumped up, and a voice shouted:

"Open the door, will yer?"

"I will directly, sir," said Oliver, beginning to turn the key.

Then the voice said through the keyhole, "I suppose yer the new boy, ain't yer?"

"Yes, sir," said Oliver.

"How old are yer?"

"Ten, sir."

"Then I'll whop yer when I get in; you just see if I don't, my workhus brat!" said the voice.

Oliver drew back the bolts with a trembling hand, and opened the door. And then he saw, sitting on a post in front of the house, a big charity boy eating a slice of bread-and-butter.

"I beg your pardon, sir," said Oliver. "Did you knock?"

"I kicked!" replied the charity boy.

"Did you want a coffin, sir?" asked Oliver innocently.

This made the charity boy very angry, for he thought Oliver was making fun of him. "Yer don't know who I am, I suppose, Workhus?" said he, climbing down from the post.

"No, sir," said Oliver.

"I'm Mister Noah Claypole; and you're under me. Take down the shutters, yer idle young ruffian."

He was a big, lumbering youth. His eyes were small, and his nose was red, and he had on yellow breeches.

Oliver took down one shutter, but it was so heavy that in his effort to lift it, he broke a pane of glass. Noah had to come to his help with the others, and he told him "he'd catch it."

And Mr. and Mrs. Sowerberry coming in soon after, Oliver did "catch it," as Noah had said. Then the two went down the flight of dark stairs to breakfast in the kitchen.

Noah was not a workhouse orphan like poor Oliver, who knew nothing of his parents. Noah's drunken father and mother lived in the town, although he had been brought up on charity. And

as the shop boys in the streets called out "Charity" after Noah, the charity boy thought it a fine thing to hurl "Workhus!" at the helpless little orphan that did not know even his father's name.

Oliver had been about three weeks at the undertaker's, when it struck Mr. Sowerberry that the boy—with his pale, handsome but sad face, would make a good mourner to attend at children's funerals; so Oliver was promoted to attend the funerals, carrying a black stick, and wearing a hat-band. This made Noah furiously jealous, and he treated Oliver worse than ever.

One day Oliver and Noah had just sat down to dinner, when Charlotte was called away. Noah immediately put his feet on the table-cloth, pulled Oliver's hair, and called him a sneak.

"Workhus," said Noah, "how's your mother?"

"She's dead," said Oliver, colouring and breathing quickly. "Don't you say anything about her to me." His mouth quivered. Noah thought he would goad him into tears.

"What did she die of, Workhus?"

"Of a broken heart, one of the old nurses told me," said Oliver. And he added, half to himself, with tears in his eyes, "I think I know what it must be to die of that."

"Yer know, Workhus," jeered Noah, yer mother was a right down bad 'un. And it's a great deal better, Workhus, that she died, or else she'd have been transported or hung."

Crimson with fury, Oliver jumped up, seized Noah by the throat, shook him till his teeth chattered in his head; and, collecting his whole force into one heavy blow, felled him to the ground.

The boy's spirit was roused at last. No one looking at him now could imagine him to be the quiet, mild, dejected child that harsh treatment had made him. The cruel insult to his dead

mother had set his blood on fire. His breast heaved; he held up his head; his eye was bright as he stood glaring over his cowardly tormentor, who now lay crouching at his feet.

"He'll murder me!" blubbered Noah. "Charlotte!—Missus!— Here's the new boy a-murdering of me! Help! Help! Oliver's gone mad!—Charlotte!"

He was answered by a loud scream from Charlotte, and a louder scream from Mrs. Sowerberry. Charlotte rushed into the kitchen. "Oh, you little wretch!" she screamed. And then with a blow from her big fist between each word, "Oh—you—little—un-grateful—murderous—horrid—villain!"

Mrs. Sowerberry plunged in, and beat him too. And the valiant Noah got up and pummelled him from behind.

Then they dragged Oliver, struggling and shouting, into the coal cellar, and locked him up.

"Oh, Charlotte!"—and Mrs. Sowerberry burst out crying— "what a mercy we have not all been murdered in our beds."

"What's to be done?" exclaimed Mrs. Sowerberry.

"Your master's not at home; there's not a man in the house, and he'll kick the door down in ten minutes."

"Dear, dear! I don't know, ma'am," said Charlotte, "unless we send for the police officers."

"No, no," said Mrs. Sowerberry. "Run to Mr. Bumble, Noah, and tell him to come directly."

Noah started off at his fullest speed, tearing through the streets pell-mell and, knocking at the gate of the workhouse, burst into the yard, shrieking, "Mr. Bumble!"

Mr. Bumble happened to be in the yard.

"Oh, Mr. Bumble, sir!" cried Noah; "Oliver has . . ."

"He hasn't run away, has he, Noah?" asked Mr. Brumble.

"No, sir, no. Not run away, sir, but he's turned vicious," said Noah. "He tried to murder me; and then he tried to murder Charlotte; and then Missus. Oh! what a dreadful pain it is! Such agony, please, sir!" and Noah writhed and twisted his body.

At that moment one of the managers came across the yard.

"It's a poor boy from the charity school, sir," replied Mr. Bumble, "who has been nearly murdered by young Oliver Twist. And," added the beadle, with a face of ashy paleness, "he has likewise attempted to murder the female servant."

"And his missus," put in Noah Claypole.

"And his master, too, you said, Noah?" added Mr. Bumble.

"No, Mr. Sowerberry was out, or he would have murdered him," replied Noah. "He said he wanted to."

"Ah! said he wanted to, did he, my boy?" said the gentleman.

"Yes, sir," replied Noah. "And please, sir, Missus wants to know whether Mr. Bumble can spare time to step up there, directly, and flog Oliver—'cause Master's out."

"Bumble," said the gentleman in the white waistcoat, "just you step up to Sowerberry's with your cane, and see what's best to be done. Don't spare him, Bumble."

"No, I will not, sir," replied the beadle; and he proceeded immediately to the scene of action.

Mrs. Sowerberry and Charlotte gave such an alarming account of Oliver's fierceness, that the beadle judged it prudent to let Oliver know who was outside the door before he opened it. So he put his mouth to the keyhole, and said in a deep, impressive voice, "Oliver!"

"Come; you let me out!" replied Oliver from the inside.

"Do you know this here voice, Oliver?" said Mr. Bumble.

"Yes," replied Oliver.

"Ain't you afraid of it, sir? Ain't you a-trembling?"

"No," replied Oliver boldly.

Mr. Bumble was staggered. He stepped back from the key-hole; drew himself up to his full height, and looked from one to another of the three bystanders in mute astonishment.

"Oh, you know, Mr. Bumble, he must be mad to speak to you so," said Mrs. Sowerberry.

"It is not Madness, ma'am," replied Mr. Bumble, after a few moments of deep thought; "it's Meat!"

"Meat!" exclaimed Mrs. Sowerberry.

"Meat, ma'am, meat. You've overfed him, ma'am. If you had kept the boy on gruel, ma'am, this would never have happened."

"Dear! dear!" tutted Mrs. Sowerberry, piously raising her eyes to the ceiling. "This comes of being liberal!" And Mrs. Sowerberry's liberality had consisted in giving to Oliver all the scraps which nobody else would eat.

"The only thing now that can be done," said Mr. Bumble, "is to leave him in the cellar for a day or two, till he's a little starved down; and then to take him out, and feed him on gruel."

At this moment Mr. Sowerberry, who had been away from home, appeared on the scene, and Mrs. Sowerberry and Charlotte repeated the story of his assault on Noah, with many additions, in the hope of rousing the undertaker's anger; because, on the whole, Mr. Sowerberry had been kind to Oliver.

The undertaker, hearing the story, opened the cellar door, and dragged his rebellious apprentice out by the collar.

"He called my mother names," explained Oliver.

"Well, and what if he did?" cried Mrs. Sowerberry. "She deserved what he said."

"She didn't," said Oliver.

"She did," said Mrs. Sowerberry.

"It's a lie," said Oliver.

Mrs. Sowerberry burst into a flood of tears

After that, Mr. Sowerberry, although kindly disposed to the boy, was obliged to give him a drubbing, and, for the rest of the day, Oliver was shut up in the back kitchen with nothing more than a slice of bread. And at night Mrs. Sowerberry looked into the room, and ordered him upstairs to his dismal bed.

He had not cried when they had beaten him, and he had listened to their taunts with a look of contempt. But now, when he found himself alone in the gloomy workshop, where none could see or hear him, Oliver fell on his knees and cried bitterly.

For a long time he knelt, then he looked round, and listened intently. Everybody had gone to bed. And then he gently undid the shop door, and looked out.

It was a cold, dark night; and the stars were shining brightly. He softly reclosed the door, and waited for the day to break.

Oliver again unbarred the door. One timid look around—one moment's pause of hesitation—then he closed the door behind him, and was in the open street.

As he ran along, he presently found himself on a road that led to Mrs. Mann's baby farm.

There was no one about. Oliver stopped, and peeped into the garden. A child was weeding one of the little beds, and as he lifted his pale face, Oliver recognized one of the little boys who had been his friend.

"Hush, Dick," said Oliver, as the boy ran to the gate and thrust his thin arm between the rails to greet him. "Is anyone up?"

"Nobody but me," replied the child.

"You mustn't say you saw me, Dick," said Oliver. "I'm running

away. They beat and ill-use me, Dick; and I'm going to seek my fortune some long way off. I don't know where. How pale you are!"

"I heard the doctor tell them I was dying," replied the child. "I'm very glad to see you, Oliver. But don't stop, don't stop."

Chapter Three
At Fagin's

Oliver started on his way, and by eight o'clock had left the town nearly five miles behind.

Later he sat down to rest by the side of a milestone, and began to wonder where he was to go, and what he was to do.

On the stone was marked "Seventy miles from London."

He jumped up then, and, as he went, he wondered how he could ever reach the place. He had a crust of bread tied up with his shirt and socks, and a penny, too, that Mr. Sowerberry had given him one day when he had been pleased with him. But what was that to help him on so long a journey in hungry winter time? He ate his crust of bread, and begged for water at the cottage doors. And when the night came, he turned into a meadow, and, creeping close up under a hayrick, he fell asleep through sheer weariness, and forgot his hunger and cold.

He was cold and stiff when he got up next morning, and so hungry that he spent his penny on a small loaf in the very first village he came to. He could not walk much that day. And another night spent in the bleak air made him so weak that he could hardly crawl along.

Indeed, if it had not been for a good-hearted turnpike man, and a benevolent old lady, Oliver must have died upon the road.

But the first gave him a meal of bread and cheese; and the old lady gave him food and shelter and money.

Early on the seventh morning Oliver limped into the little town of Barnet, and sat down upon a doorstep.

No one took any notice of him except a boy who crossed the road and came up to Oliver.

He was a dirty, snub-nosed boy, short, with bow legs, and little, sharp, ugly eyes—with all the airs and manners of a man. He wore a man's coat which reached to his heels, with the cuffs turned back half-way up his arms; and a hat on his head.

"I'm very hungry and tired," said Oliver, with tears in his eyes. "I have walked a long way. I have been walking seven days."

"Walking for sivin days!" said the boy.

With that he helped Oliver to rise, and took him to a shop where he bought some ham and bread.

"Going to London?" asked the strange boy.

"Yes."

"Got any lodgings?"

"No."

"Money?"

"No," repeated Oliver.

"Do you live in London?" asked Oliver.

"I do when I'm at home," replied the boy. "I suppose you want some place to sleep in tonight, don't you?"

"I do indeed," said Oliver. "I haven't slept under a roof since I left the country."

After that the two had a confidential talk, the strange boy saying that his name was Jack Dawkins, and that he was known among his intimate friends as "The Artful Dodger." He also

spoke highly of an old gentleman who would befriend Oliver, and get him a comfortable place by-and-by.

Oliver was much relieved, and, needless to say, was very willing to go to London with Master Jack Dawkins. It was eleven o'clock when they reached the great City, and, after leading Oliver through all sorts of side streets, they at last turned down a very narrow, dirty, ill-smelling one, full of small shops.

The Dodger caught him by the arm, pushed open the door of a house, and pulled him into the passage.

The Dodger whistled, and a voice called out, "Now then!"

"Plummy and slam!" returned the Dodger.

A light gleamed in the distance, and a man's face appeared.

"There's two of you," said the man. "Who's the t'other one?"

"A new pal," replied the Dodger, pulling Oliver forward.

"Where did he come from?"

"From Greenland," answered the Dodger. "Is Fagin upstairs?"

"Yes," was the reply. "He's sortin' the wipes. Up with you!" The candle was drawn back, and the face disappeared.

Oliver, groping his way with one hand, and having the other firmly grasped by his companion, climbed the dark and broken stairs, and soon they got into a dirty room where a very shrivelled old man with a villainous face—almost hidden in a quantity of matted red hair—was toasting sausages over the fire.

There were a lot of silk handkerchiefs hanging on a clothes-horse; and several rough beds made of old sacks on the floor; and round the table were four or five boys, not any older than the Dodger.

The Dodger whispered to the man, and all the boys turned round and grinned at Oliver.

"This is him, Fagin," said the Dodger. "My friend Oliver Twist."

Fagin shook hands very heartily, and so did the boys.

"We are very glad to see you, Oliver, very," said Fagin. "Dodger, take off the sausages, and draw a tub near the fire for our guest. Ah! I see you're a-staring at the pocket-handkerchiefs, eh, my dear? There are a good many of them, ain't there? We've just looked 'em out, ready for the wash."

At that all the boys laughed boisterously, and soon the whole party sat down to supper. Oliver ate his share, and then Fagin mixed him a glass of hot gin and water, and told him to drink it off directly, as another gentleman wanted the tumbler. Oliver did as he was bid. Immediately he felt himself gently lifted on to one of the sacks; and then he sank into a deep sleep.

Oliver opened his eyes next morning after a long, long sleep. There was no one in the room but Fagin, who was boiling coffee in a saucepan and whistling softly to himself. He saw Fagin take a small box from a trap in the floor, and out of that he took a magnificent gold watch, sparkling with jewels.

He took out other boxes from which he took rings, and brooches, and bracelets, and other jewellery; gloating over them as he held each in his hand.

Then he put these away, and took up a tiny trinket, which he had to examine very closely.

Turning suddenly, he saw Oliver's eyes fixed upon him. Fagin shut down the lid of the box with a loud crash. And laying his hand on a bread-knife which was on the table, he started up furiously, trembling with passion. In his terror, Oliver could see the knife quivering in the air.

"What's that? "said Fagin. "What do you watch me for? Why are you awake? What have you seen? Speak out, boy! Quick—quick!—for your life!"

"I wasn't able to sleep any longer, sir," replied Oliver, meekly.

"You were not awake an hour ago?" said Fagin, scowling fiercely on the boy.

"No! No, indeed!" replied Oliver.

"Are you sure?" cried Fagin, with a still fiercer look.

"Upon my word I was not, sir," replied Oliver, earnestly.

"Tush, tush, my dear!" said Fagin, resuming his old manner, and toying with the knife a little, as if to show Oliver he had only been in play. "Of course I know that. I only tried to frighten you. Ha, ha! you're a brave boy, Oliver." And he tried to pass it off with a chuckle; but he glanced uneasily at the box as he did so.

"Did you see anything of these pretty things, my dear?" he asked after a pause, laying his hand upon the box.

"Yes, sir," said Oliver.

Fagin turned a little pale. "They're mine, Oliver. My little property. All I have to live on in my old age."

Soon, Dodger returned with one of the other boys, whom he now introduced as Charley Bates. Then the four sat down to breakfast on the coffee, with some hot rolls and ham which the Dodger had brought home in the crown of his hat.

"Well," said Fagin, glancing slyly at Oliver, and addressing himself to the Dodger, "I hope you've been at work this morning, my dears?"

"Hard," replied the Dodger.

"As nails," added Charley Bates.

"Good boys," said Fagin. "What have you got, Dodger?"

"A couple of pocket-books," replied that young gentleman.

"Lined?" inquired Fagin with eagerness.

"Pretty well," replied the Dodger, producing two pocket-books—one green, and the other red.

"Not so heavy as they might be," said Fagin, after looking at the inside carefully; "but very neat, and nicely made. Clever workman, ain't he, Oliver?"

"Very, indeed, sir," said Oliver.

"And what have you got, my dear?" said Fagin to Charley Bates.

"Wipes," replied Master Bates; at the same time producing four pocket-handkerchiefs.

When the breakfast was cleared away, the merry old gentleman and the two boys played a curious game. Fagin put a snuffbox in one pocket, a note-case in the other, a diamond pin in his shirt, and a watch in his waistcoat pocket, with a guard chain round his neck, and trotted up and down the room like any old gentleman in the street.

Sometimes he stopped to look into the fire, and sometimes at the door, making-believe that he was staring in at shop windows. At such times he would look constantly round him for fear of thieves, and would slap his pockets in turn to see if he had lost anything, in such a funny and natural manner, that Oliver laughed till the tears ran down his face.

And all the time the two boys followed Fagin about very nimbly, till at last the Dodger trod upon his toes, while Charley Bates stumbled up against him from behind; and in that moment they took from him, with extraordinary rapidity, the snuff-box, note-case, chain, shirt-pin, and pocket-handkerchief.

If Fagin felt a hand in his pocket, he cried out where it was; and then the game began again. They were to take the articles away without his feeling anything.

By-and-by two young women, with rather untidy hair, came to call upon Fagin. One was called Bet, the other Nancy. They were stout, hearty-looking girls, and very free and agreeable in

their manners. Fagin gave them each a drink of gin; and by-and-by he gave them money too. And then Charley Bates and the Dodger went out with the girls.

"There, my dear," said Fagin, "that's a pleasant life, isn't it? They have gone out for the day."

"Have they gone to work, sir?" asked Oliver.

"Yes," answered Fagin. And then he added, "Make 'em your models, my dear. Make 'em your models. Do everything they bid you, and take their advice in all matters, especially the Dodger's… Is my handkerchief hanging out of my pocket, my dear?" he asked, stopping short.

"Yes, sir," said Oliver.

"See if you can take it out without my feeling it, as you saw them do when we were at play this morning."

Oliver held up the bottom of the pocket with one hand, as he had seen the Dodger hold it, and drew the handkerchief lightly out of it with the other.

"Is it gone?" cried Fagin.

"Here it is, sir," said Oliver, showing it in his hand.

"You're a clever boy, my dear," said the playful old gentleman, patting Oliver on the head. "I never saw a sharper lad."

As time went on Oliver was astonished to find that such steady and hard-working boys behaved so badly in the street. They kept on snatching up an apple or an onion off the corners of the stalls they passed, doing it so quickly, too, that the owners never caught them as they did it. They also loitered about the street, instead of hurrying to their work, and Oliver began to think they were not the steady boys Fagin seemed to think they were.

Suddenly, the Dodger drew Charley's attention towards an old

gentleman who was standing over a bookstall, diligently reading a book that he had picked up.

He was a very respectable-looking personage, with a powdered head and gold spectacles. He was dressed in a bottle-green coat with a black velvet collar; wore white trousers, and carried a smart bamboo cane under his arm.

Charley Bates said he was "a prime plant." And the two boys immediately crossed the road, and slunk close behind the old gentleman.

And then Oliver saw the Dodger put his hand into the old gentleman's pocket, and draw from it a handkerchief. This he handed to Charley Bates, and in a moment away the boys tore, as hard as they could, round the corner.

In an instant the whole mystery of the handkerchiefs, and the watches, and the jewels, and Fagin, was revealed to Oliver. The boys were thieves; and *the work they did was thieving!* With the blood mounting into his face, confused and frightened, Oliver took to his heels. At that very moment the old gentleman, putting his hand into his pocket for his handkerchief, missed it, and, turning, he saw Oliver scudding away as hard as he could.

"Stop thief!" shouted the old gentleman, and made after him with all his might.

As for the Dodger and Charley Bates, they had merely turned into the first doorway round the corner. And when they heard the cry "Stop thief!" and saw Oliver running, they guessed exactly how it had come about, and they also shouted "Stop thief!" and joined in the pursuit.

And soon the cry was taken up by a hundred voices, and pell-mell, helter-skelter the people tore after Oliver. He ran on; terror in his looks; agony in his eyes; large drops of perspiration

streaming down his face; till a blow from somebody threw him to the pavement, and the crowd eagerly gathered round.

"Where's the gentleman?" somebody cried.

"Here he is, coming down the street."

"Is this the boy, sir?"

"Yes," said the old gentleman, "I'm afraid it is the boy." And he looked quite sorry that Oliver had been caught.

But before he could say anything more, a policeman made his way through the crowd, and seized Oliver by the collar.

"It wasn't me, indeed, sir. Indeed, it was two other boys," said Oliver, clasping his hands passionately, and looking round.

"Don't hurt him," cried the old gentleman compassionately.

"Oh no, I won't hurt him," said the policeman. And he dragged Oliver away by the collar, while the old gentleman walked by his side, and a crowd of boys followed, shouting triumphantly.

"I would rather not press the case," said the old gentleman anxiously, when they got to the police court. But they told him that the case must go before the magistrate now.

The old gentleman looked quite unhappy when Oliver was locked up, and, turning with a sigh to his book, which had been the innocent cause of all this disturbance, he said to himself, "There is something in that boy's face that touches and interests me. *Can* he be innocent? He looked like ... By-the-bye, bless my soul! where have I seen something like that look before?"

The magistrate sat behind the bar at the upper end of the office; and on one side of the door was a sort of wooden pen in which poor Oliver was standing, trembling at the awfulness of his position.

The magistrate was a bad-tempered man, and listened to what the old gentleman said very impatiently indeed.

As for Oliver, he was so frightened that he could not utter a sound when he was questioned; and he fainted in the court.

Just then a man came rushing breathlessly into the court, who demanded to be sworn, saying that he had seen it all, and had now come up to speak for Oliver.

He turned out to be the bookstall keeper himself; and he told the magistrate how he had seen two other boys take the handkerchief from the old gentleman's pocket, and how Oliver had run through sheer fright.

"Clear the office," shouted the magistrate, dismissing the case.

And when Mr. Brownlow—the old gentleman who had been robbed—came out, he saw Oliver Twist lying on the pavement with his shirt unbuttoned, his face deadly white, and a cold tremble convulsing his whole frame.

"Poor boy, poor boy!" said Mr. Brownlow, bending over him. "Call a coach, somebody, pray. Directly!"

A coach was got, and Oliver was carefully laid on one seat, the old gentleman then got in and off they drove.

Chapter Four
Oliver Finds a Friend

The coach rattled away till they stopped at last before a neat house, in a quiet shady street, near Pentonville. Here a bed was prepared by kind hands, in which Oliver was gently laid, and tended with a care that knew no bounds.

But for many days Oliver, tossing with fever, remained insensible to all the goodness of his new friends, till at last he awoke.

"What room is this?" asked Oliver feebly, raising himself on his arm. "This is not the place I went to sleep in."

"Hush, my dear," said a motherly old woman, looking round the curtain. "You must be very quiet, or you'll be ill again. Lie down again, there's a dear!" With these words she gently placed Oliver's head on the pillow, smoothed back his hair, and looked so kindly into his face that he could not help placing his little wasted hand in hers, and drawing it round his neck.

"Save us!" said the old woman, with tears in her eyes. "What a grateful little dear it is! Pretty creetur! What would his mother feel if she had sat by him as I have, and could see him now!"

The old woman, brought something for Oliver to drink, and told him to lie very quiet, or he would be ill again.

So Oliver, anxious to please this kind person, lay very quiet, and soon fell into a gentle doze. And when he awoke again, there was a light in the room, and an old gentleman, with a large, loud-ticking gold watch in his hand, was feeling his pulse.

This was the doctor, who spoke very kindly too, and told the old woman—whom he called Mrs. Bedwin—to give his patient some tea and dry toast.

In three days' time Oliver was able to sit in an easy-chair, propped up with pillows; and as he was still too weak to walk, Mrs. Bedwin had him carried down to her own little room, and Oliver learned that she was Mr. Brownlow's housekeeper.

"You're very, very kind to me, ma'am," said Oliver.

"Well, never you mind that, my dear," said the old woman; "that's got nothing to do with your broth. And it's full time you had it, for the doctor says Mr. Brownlow may come in to see you this morning; and you must get up your best looks, because the better you look, the more he'll be pleased."

So Oliver drank his broth, and thought he had never tasted anything so good before.

Then Mrs. Bedwin asked him if he was fond of pictures; as Oliver was staring hard at the portrait of a lady on the wall.

"I don't know," said Oliver. "I have seen so few that I hardly know. What a beautiful face that lady's is!"

And while they were talking, there was a rap at the door.

"Come in," said Mrs. Bedwin. And in walked Mr. Brownlow.

"Poor boy," said Mr. Brownlow. "Have you given him any nourishment, Bedwin? Any slops, eh?"

"He has had a basin of strong broth, sir," said Mrs. Bedwin.

"A couple of glasses of port wine would have done him a great deal more good," returned the old gentleman. And then he cried suddenly, "Why! what's this? Bedwin, look there!"

And he pointed hastily to the picture of the lady Oliver had admired, and then to the boy's face. There was its living copy. The eyes, the head, the mouth—every feature was the same.

Mr. Brownlow had cried out so suddenly that it gave Oliver a start, and, being still very weak, he just fainted away. But he soon recovered under Mrs. Bedwin's care.

The fainting fit had thrown him back a little, though, and he could not get up to breakfast the next morning. And when he came down again to the housekeeper's room, he was disappointed that the picture of the lady had been removed.

When he grew well enough to put on his clothes, Mr. Brownlow had a new suit ordered for him, and a new cap, and a new pair of shoes. They were the first new things Oliver ever had.

And now we must go back for a few minutes to the Dodger and Charley Bates. It caused that last-named young gentleman great merriment to think that Oliver had been suspected of being the thief, when he himself had the stolen handkerchief in his own pocket all the time.

But the Artful Dodger put a stop to Master Bates's laughter by asking, "What'll Fagin say?"

Fagin was sitting over the fire when he heard their feet upon the creaking stairs; and, as he listened, his face changed. "Only two of 'em," he muttered. "Where's the third? They can't have got into trouble."

The footsteps reached the landing. The door was slowly opened and the Dodger and Charley Bates entered.

"Where's Oliver?" cried Fagin. "Where's the boy?"

"The traps have got him, and that's all about it," said the Dodger sullenly. "Come, let go of me, will you!" And, swinging free, he seized the toasting-fork, and threatened Fagin with it.

Fagin stepped back and seized the pewter pot, and was going to fling it at the Dodger, when Charley Bates set up a terrific howl, and so Fagin flung it at Bates instead of at the Dodger.

"Why, what the blazes is in the wind now?" growled a deep voice at the door. "Who pitched that at me? It's well it's the beer and not the pot as hit me. Wot's it all about, Fagin?"

The man who growled out these words was a stoutly built fellow of about thirty-five, in a black velveteen coat, dirty drab breeches, laced-up half boots, and grey cotton stockings, which enclosed a bulky pair of legs with large swelling calves. He had a brown hat on his head, and a pair of scowling eye.

"Come in, d'ye hear?" growled the ruffian. And a white shaggy dog skulked into the room.

"What are you up to? Ill-treating the boys, you covetous, avaricious old fence?" said the man, seating himself deliberately.

"Hush, hush, Mr. Sikes!" said Fagin, trembling.

"None of your mistering," replied the ruffian. "You know my name: out with it! I shan't disgrace it when the time comes."

"Well, well, then, Bill Sikes," said Fagin with abject humility. "You seem out of humour, Bill."

"Perhaps I am," replied Sikes. And then he demanded a glass of gin, adding—"Mind you don't poison it."

After swallowing two or three glasses of spirits, Mr. Sikes condescended to take some notice of the boys. And then the story of Oliver's capture was related by the Dodger.

"I'm afraid," said Fagin, "that he may say something which will get us into trouble."

"That's very likely," returned Sikes, with a malicious grin. "You're blowed upon, Fagin."

"And I'm afraid, you see," added Fagin, regarding the other closely as he spoke, "that if the game was up with us, it might be up with a good many more, and that it would come out rather worse for you than it would for me."

"Somebody must find out wot's been done at the office," said Sikes, in a much lower tone than he had taken since he came in.

Fagin nodded.

"If he hasn't peached, and is sent to prison, there's no fear till he comes out again," said Sikes. "And then he must be taken care of. You must get hold of him somehow."

It was very important that they should get hold of Oliver again. But, unfortunately, one and all objected strongly to going near a police office to make inquiries as to what had become of him.

And as they sat looking at each other, Nancy and Bet, the two cheerful young women, walked into the room.

"The very thing!" said Fagin. "Bet will go, won't you, my dear?"

"Where?" inquired the young lady.

"Only just up to the office, my dear," said Fagin coaxingly.

Bet said she would be "blessed" if she did.

"Nancy, my dear," said Fagin to the other girl, "what do *you* say?"

"That it won't do; so it's no use a-trying it on, Fagin."

Then followed a lot of discussion. And in the end Nancy at last agreed to go, for, as it happened, she was not so well known at the police office as were the other members of the gang.

So Fagin immediately produced a clean white apron and a straw bonnet for Nancy to wear. "Stop a minute, my dear," said he, giving her a little covered basket. "Carry that in one hand. It looks more respectable, my dear."

Nancy found her way to the police office, where she inquired, with many tears and piteous wailings, as to the welfare of her own dear little brother Nolly.

The police officer, told her how Oliver had been discharged because a witness had come up at the last moment and proved that the robbery was committed by another boy; and that the gentleman who had prosecuted Oliver had carried him away.

Nancy wrung her hands, and staggered to the gate. But as soon as she got out of sight of the police court, she ran off as hard as she could to Fagin's.

"We must know where he is, my dear. He must be found," cried the excited Fagin.

Bill Sikes snatched up his hat, whistled to the dog, and disappeared like lightning.

"Charley," said the trembling Fagin, "do nothing but skulk about till you bring home some news of him! Nancy, my dear, I must have him found. I trust to you, my dear—to you and the Artful—for everything! Stay, stay!" he added, "there's money, my dears," unlocking a drawer with a shaking hand. "I shall shut up this shop tonight. You'll know where to find me! Don't stop up here a minute. Not an instant, my dears!"

Then he pushed them from the room, and, first locking the door behind them, he drew from its hiding-place the box of beautiful jewels Oliver had seen that first day.

A noise at the door startled him. But it was only the Dodger speaking through the keyhole to ask whether Oliver should be taken to their other den, if they should catch him.

Fagin answered, "Yes. Find him, find him out—that's all! I shall know what to do next."

It was just a week since Oliver had left his room. He had grown in Mrs. Bedwin's good graces. "A grateful, affectionate child," she called him. And Oliver felt he could have done anything for this good woman—the kindest he had ever met in his life.

Mr. Brownlow sent for him one evening, and talked to him very kindly, too; and told him that he was willing and anxious to help him in his future life. "You need not be afraid of my deserting you," he said, "unless you give me cause. I have been deceived before," added the old gentleman, "in the objects whom I have tried to benefit. But I feel strongly inclined to trust you, nevertheless." And then he asked Oliver to tell him his story, and to speak the truth.

Oliver had just begun to tell him about Mrs. Mann's baby farm, and Mr. Bumble, and the workhouse, when another old gentleman suddenly appeared on a visit to Mr. Brownlow. His name was Mr. Grimwig.

"This is young Oliver Twist, whom we were speaking about," said Mr. Brownlow.

"How are you, boy?" said Mr. Grimwig, after staring hard at Oliver suspiciously.

"A great deal better, thank you, sir," replied Oliver.

The old gentleman looked more suspicious than ever; so Mr.

Brownlow told Oliver to step down and tell Mrs. Bedwin that they were ready for tea.

And Mr. Grimwig took the opportunity to hint that Mr. Brownlow's goodness would be wasted on the boy.

Mr. Brownlow immediately took Oliver's part. And because Mr. Grimwig was an aggravating old gentleman, and a very contradictory one, he at once declared that Oliver would deceive his good friend one day.

Now, while they were talking, a parcel of books was brought in by Mrs. Bedwin, that had just come from the bookseller's.

"Stop the boy, Mrs. Bedwin!" said Mr. Brownlow; "there are some books to be taken back."

But the boy had gone. And though Oliver ran one way and the servant ran another, they could not find him.

"Dear me, I am very sorry for that," exclaimed Mr. Brownlow. "I particularly wished those books to be returned tonight."

"Send Oliver with them," said Mr. Grimwig, with an ironical smile. "He will be sure to deliver them safely, you know."

And Oliver, delighted, said, "I'll run all the way, sir."

Mr. Brownlow was going to say No, when Mr. Grimwig coughed aggravatingly, as much as to say he would not trust him.

"You shall go, my dear," said Mr. Brownlow. "The books are on a chair by my table. Fetch them down."

Oliver brought down the books under his arm, and waited, cap in hand, to hear what message he had to take.

"You are to say," said Mr. Brownlow, glancing steadily at Mr. Grimwig, "that you have brought these books back; and that you have come to pay the four pound ten I owe him. This is a five-pound note; so you will have to bring me back ten shillings change."

"I won't be ten minutes, sir," said Oliver eagerly. And he buttoned up the bank-note in his jacket pocket, and carried the books under his arm.

Mrs. Bedwin followed him to the street door, giving him many directions about the nearest way, and the name of the bookseller, and told him also to be sure and not take cold.

"Bless his sweet face," said the old woman, looking after him. "I can't bear, somehow, to let him out of my sight."

"Let me see: he'll be back in twenty minutes at the longest," said Mr. Brownlow, pulling out his watch.

"Oh, you really expect him to come back, do you?" inquired Mr. Grimwig.

"Don't you?" asked Mr. Brownlow, smiling.

"No," returned Mr. Grimwig, hitting the table with his fist. "I do not. The boy has got a new suit of clothes on his back, a set of valuable books under his arm, and a five-pound note in his pocket. He'll join his old friends the thieves, and laugh at you. If ever that boy returns to this house, sir, I'll eat my head."

With these words he drew his chair closer to the table. And there the two friends sat in silent expectation, with the watch between them.

Chapter Five
With Fagin Again

Meanwhile, Oliver Twist, having reached Clerkenwell, accidentally turned down a by-street, which was not exactly in his way. He was thinking how happy he was, when he got startled by a young woman screaming out, "Oh, my dear brother!" And he was stopped by having a pair of arms thrown round his neck.

"Don't," cried Oliver, struggling. "Let me go. Who is it? What are you stopping me for?"

"Why, it's Nancy!" cried Oliver, who now saw her face for the first time. And he started back astonished and afraid.

At that moment a man rushed out of a beershop, with a white dog at his heels. "What's this? Young Oliver! Come home to your poor mother, you young dog. Come home directly."

It was Bill Sikes.

"Yes, I'll help you, you young rascal. What books are these? You've been stealing 'em, have you?" And Sikes wrenched them from his hand, and hit him on the head.

"That's right!" cried an onlooker. "That's the only way of bringing him to his senses."

Bill Sikes seized Oliver by the collar. Oliver was dragged along through narrow streets.

They walked on for half-an-hour, until they turned into a very narrow street, full of old-clothes shops. And then they stopped before the door of a shop that was closed.

"All right," said Sikes, looking cautiously round.

Nancy stooped below the shutters, and Oliver heard the sound of a bell. They crossed to the opposite side of the street, and stood for a few minutes under a lamp. A noise, as if the sash of a window was gently raised, was heard; and by-and-by the door was softly opened. Sikes seized the terrified boy by the collar, and all three were quickly inside the house.

They crossed an empty kitchen; and—opening the door of a low earth-smelling room, which seemed to have been built in a back yard—were received with a shout of laughter.

"Oh, my!" cried Charley Bates. "Here he is! Oh, Fagin, look at him! Fagin, do look at him. Hold me, while I laugh."

Fagin took off his night-cap and bowed low to the boy. And the Artful Dodger set about rifling his pockets.

"Delighted to see you looking so well, my dear," said Fagin. "The Artful shall give you another suit, for fear you should spoil that Sunday one. Why didn't you write, my dear, and say you were coming? We'd have got something warm for supper."

At this Charley Bates roared again. And suddenly the Artful drew forth the five-pound note.

"Hullo! what's that?" inquired Sikes, as Fagin seized the note. "That's mine, Fagin."

"No, no my dear," said Fagin. "Mine, Bill, mine. You shall have the books."

Bill Sikes plucked the note from between Fagin's finger and thumb; and, looking the old man coolly in the face, folded it up small and tied it in his neckerchief

"That's for our share of the trouble," said Sikes. "And not half enough, neither. You may keep the books, if you're fond of reading. If you ain't, sell 'em."

Oliver wrung his hands. "They belong to the old gentleman— to the good, kind old gentleman who took me into his house, and had me nursed, when I was near dying of the fever. Oh, pray send them back! Send him back the books and the money. Keep me here all my life long; but pray, pray send them back. He'll think I stole them. Oh, do have mercy on me, and send them back!" And Oliver fell on his knees at Fagin's feet, and beat his hands together in an agony of desperation.

Fagin looked slyly round. "You're right, Oliver, you're right. They *will* think you've stolen 'em. Ha, ha!" he chuckled, rubbing his hands, "it couldn't have happened better."

"Of course it couldn't," replied Sikes.

Oliver looked from one to the other. Jumping suddenly to his feet, he ran from the room, crying for help but he was caught almost immediately.

Fagin addressed Oliver. "Wanted to get assistance? Called for the police, did you?" he snarled. And, lifting a knotted club near the fireplace, he brought it down on Oliver's shoulder, and was raising it for a second blow, when Nancy rushed forward, snatched it from his hand, and flung it into the fire.

"I won't stand by and see it done, Fagin," said the girl. "You've got the boy, and what more would you have? Let him be—let him be—or I shall put that mark on some of you, that will bring me to the gallows before my time."

The men stared at one another in a perplexed manner. Fagin spoke soothingly; and Sikes began to swear. But it had no effect on Nancy in her recklessness and despair. She was not altogether bad, and deep down in her heart she hated herself for having brought poor Oliver back to Fagin.

Master Bates led Oliver into the next room, where the boys' beds were, and, helping him to take off the new suit Mr. Brownlow had ordered for him, Charley Bates tucked them under his arm, saying that he would give them to Fagin to take care of. And, leaving Oliver in the dark, he locked the door behind him.

Oliver heard their noisy laughter from the next room. But he was sick and weary. And he soon fell asleep.

So Mr. Grimwig, the suspicious old gentleman, was right, and Oliver did not come back after all.

By-and-by, Mr. Brownlow, still anxious for the boy's welfare, and wishing to think the best of him, put this advertisement into the paper:—

FIVE GUINEAS REWARD

Whereas a young boy, named Oliver Twist, ran away, or was enticed, on Thursday evening last, from his home at Pentonville; and has not since been heard of. The above reward will be paid to any person who will give such information as will lead to the discovery of the said Oliver Twist, or tend to throw any light upon his previous history, in which the advertiser is, for many reasons, warmly interested.

And then followed a full description of Oliver's dress, person, and appearance; with the name and address of Mr. Brownlow.

And who saw that advertisement? No less a person than Mr. Bumble the beadle, who had come up to London on a little business for the workhouse.

He read it three times. And in less than five minutes was on his way to Pentonville; and he had no sooner mentioned Oliver's name, than he was ushered immediately into the little study where sat Mr. Brownlow and his suspicious friend Mr. Grimwig, with decanters and glasses before them.

Both the old gentlemen were very much excited, and soon Mr. Bumble was, much to his satisfaction, recounting all he knew of Oliver's life—a foundling, born in the workhouse of low and vicious parents, as he said; that he was also a bad, ungrateful boy, who had run away from his master's house one night, after a cowardly attack on Noah Claypole, the charity boy.

"I fear it is all too true," said Mr. Brownlow, very sorrowfully. "I would gladly have given you treble the money if your news had been favourable to the boy."

Mr. Bumble pocketed the five guineas that Mr. Brownlow laid on the table, and shook his head; and felt very sorry indeed that he had not known earlier that the gentleman would have given

three times that amount if he had spoken well of Oliver. But it was too late now.

When the beadle had gone, Mr. Brownlow walked up and down, and looked so much disturbed, that even Mr. Grimwig said nothing more.

Then Mr. Brownlow rang the bell. "Mrs. Bedwin," he said, when the housekeeper appeared, "that boy Oliver is an impostor."

"We have just had a full account of him from his birth; and he has been a little villain all his life."

"I never will believe it, sir," replied Mrs. Bedwin firmly. "Never! He was a dear, grateful, gentle child, sir,"

"Silence!" said Mr. Brownlow. "Never let me hear the boy's name again.

Mrs. Bedwin's heart was sorrowful that night, and Mr. Brownlow's heart was sorrowful too.

Chapter Six
Fagin's Warning

The next day, Fagin gave Oliver a long lecture. The child's blood ran cold as he listened to his dark threats.

Then Fagin smiled, and, patting Oliver on the head, said that he saw plainly they would become good friends yet. And, putting on an old, battered greatcoat, he went out, locking the door behind him.

For many days Oliver remained locked up.

So lonely was he sometimes, that he would crouch in the passage by the street door to be as near to living people as he could; and he would remain there, listening, until Fagin or the boys returned.

One afternoon the Dodger sat while Oliver cleaned the Dodger's boots.

"Why don't you put yourself under Fagin, Oliver?" he urged.

"I don't like it," said Oliver. "I wish they would let me go."

"And Fagin would *rather* you didn't."

Oliver knew that well. Fagin feared that the whole gang would be pounced upon by the police, if any outsider got hold of Oliver to question him. He knew better than to let Oliver go.

"Why, where's your spirit?" asked the Dodger. "Don't you take any pride out of yourself? Would you go and be dependent on your friends?"

"That's too mean, that is," said Charley Bates going in, drawing two or three silk handkerchiefs from his pocket, and tossing them into a cupboard.

"*I* couldn't do it," said the Dodger, with an air of disgust.

"You can leave your friends, though," said Oliver, with a half smile, "and let them be punished for what you did."

"That," said the Dodger, with a wave of his pipe, "that was out of consideration for Fagin, 'cause the traps know that we work together. And we might have got into trouble, if we hadn't run. Look here," added the Dodger, drawing forth a handful of shillings and halfpence. "Here's a jolly life! What's the odds where it comes from? Here, catch hold! There's plenty more where they were took from."

"And," said the Dodger, "you've just as good a right to them as they have."

"To be sure, to be sure," said Fagin, entering at that moment. "It all lies in a nutshell, my dear. Take the Dodger's word for it. Ha! ha! ha!" and the old man rubbed his hands together, and chuckled with delight at his pupil's cleverness.

After this, Oliver was not so much alone; and the boys and Fagin often played the old game together.

Fagin was kind, too, in his way, and kept on explaining to Oliver all the advantages of his trade. Often, sitting over the fire with the three boys, he would tell them stories of robberies he had committed in his younger days, mixed up with so much that was funny and curious, that Oliver could not help laughing heartily with the other boys.

Indeed, the wary old man made his stories as interesting and as laughable as possible, only for Oliver's sake. "Once let him feel that he is one of us," thought the wily old man; "once let him steal; and he is mine!—mine for life!"

And then, one chill, damp night Fagin went to see Bill Sikes about a big robbery that they were planning at a large country house. The place was barred up at night like a jail, Sikes said, and the only way of getting in safely was through a little lattice window at the back of the house—so small that only a very little boy could manage to squeeze through.

Fagin rubbed his dirty hands together, and, in a hoarse voice, suggested Oliver.

"He's just the size I want," said Sikes, considering.

"And will do everything you want, Bill, my dear," said Fagin. "He can't help himself. That is, if you frighten him enough."

"Frighten him!" echoed Sikes. "If there's anything strange about him when we once get into work;—in for a penny, in for a pound. You won't see him alive again, Fagin."

"I've thought of it all," said Fagin. "I've had my eye upon him close—close. Once let him feel that he is one of us; once fill his mind with the idea that he has been a thief, and he's ours!—Ours for life! It couldn't have come about better!"

"And wot," said Sikes, scowling fiercely on him, "wot makes you take so much pains about one chalk-faced kid, when you know there's fifty boys about Covent Garden every night, as you might pick and choose from."

"Because they're of no use to me," replied Fagin, with some confusion—"not worth the taking. Their looks convict 'em when they get into trouble, and I lose 'em all. With this boy, properly managed, I could do what I couldn't with twenty of 'em. Now, when is it to be done, Bill?"

"I planned with Toby the night arter tomorrow, if he heerd nothing from me to the contrairy."

"Good," said Fagin; "there's no moon."

When Oliver awoke in the morning, he was a good deal surprised to find that a new pair of shoes, with strong thick soles, had been placed at his bedside.

His heart beat quickly. The shoes looked as if they were to be worn in the streets. He was to go out at last. And then Fagin told him that he was to be taken that night to Bill Sikes's house.

Nancy came for Oliver late that evening. A hackney-cab was waiting for them. Nancy pulled Oliver in with her, and drew the curtains close. The driver wanted no instructions, but drove away in an instant, and pulled up his horse at Sikes's house.

For one brief moment, Oliver cast a hurried glance along the empty street, ready to cry for help as they got out of the cab; but Nancy was whispering in his ear that to shout for help would be to injure her; and this she did in such a voice of agony that Oliver had not the heart to make the attempt.

"If I could help you, I would," she added, "but I have not the power. They don't mean to harm you. Whatever they make you do, it is no fault of yours."

And while Oliver hesitated, the opportunity was gone. He was already in the house, and the door was shut.

"This way," said the girl, letting his hand go for the first time.

"So you've got the kid," said Sikes, when they reached the room, closing the door as he spoke.

"Yes, here he is," replied Nancy.

"Did he come quiet?" inquired Sikes.

"Like a lamb."

"I'm glad to hear it," said Sikes, looking grimly at Oliver, "for the sake of his own carcase. Come here, young 'un."

Then he took the trembling boy by the shoulder, and showed him a pocket pistol, loading it carefully in front of Oliver, and putting the barrel close to the boy's temple.

"If you speak a word," said Sikes, "when you are out of doors with me, except when I speak to you, that loading will be in your head, without notice. So if you *do* make up your mind to speak without leave, say your prayers first. D'ye hear me?"

After that Bill Sikes demanded supper, so Nancy went out, and came back in a few minutes with a pot of porter and a dish of sheep's heads. Mr. Sikes made a hearty meal, but it is needless to say that poor Oliver had not much appetite.

Then Sikes ordered Nancy to wake him at five o'clock precisely, and told Oliver to lie down on a mattress on the floor. Then he went to bed himself.

When he awoke it was not yet daylight, for the candle was still burning; but Nancy was preparing an early breakfast.

"Now then," growled Sikes, as Oliver started up. "Half-past five. Look sharp, or you'll get no breakfast!"

Chapter Seven
With the Burglars

It was a cheerless morning when they got into the street. It was blowing, and raining hard; and the clouds looked dull and stormy.

Sikes tramped along without a word, holding Oliver's hand.

"Now, young 'un, you must step out. Come, don't lag behind already, lazy-legs."

Oliver, between a fast walk and a run, kept up with the rapid strides of the house-breaker as well as he could.

They passed Hyde Park Corner, and were now on their way to Kensington, when Sikes relaxed his pace, and seeing an empty cart coming their way, he asked the driver very civilly if he would give him a lift.

The man told them to jump up.

They passed Kensington, Hammersmith, Chiswick, Kew Bridge, and Brentford. At last they came to a public-house, and here the cart stopped.

Sikes jumped down hurriedly, lifted Oliver down with the same warning glance, and said goodbye to the man. Then, after a little more walking, he turned into an old public-house, where Sikes ordered cold meat for dinner and Oliver fell asleep.

When he woke up it was quite dark, and he found that Sikes had arranged for another lift in a cart going his way. Sikes took his hand and helped him up, and off they started in a few moments. It was very dark and very cold, and Oliver sat huddled together in a corner of the cart.

After a long drive Sikes got down once more, and, after a tedious walk through mud and darkness, he turned into a solitary

house, all ruinous and decayed. The house was in darkness too; but when Sikes softly pressed the latch, the door opened, and they went in together.

"Hullo?" cried a loud, hoarse voice, as soon as they had got into the passage.

"Don't make such a row," said Sikes, bolting the door.

"Aha! my pal," cried the same voice.

Sikes pushed Oliver in front of him, and they entered a low, dark room with a smoky fire, two or three broken chairs, a table, and an old sofa. On the sofa, stretched at full length, was a flashily dressed individual with reddish hair, his dirty fingers ornamented with large common rings.

This was Mr. Toby Crackit—Flash Toby Crackit, as he was known among the gang; and he was going to help Sikes with the big robbery in which Oliver was to take part.

"Bill, my boy, I'm glad to see you," said Mr. Toby Crackit. "I was almost afraid you'd given it up, in which case I would have made a venture myself." And then, he stared hard at Oliver.

Sikes explained. And then he demanded food to put some heart into them, adding to Oliver, "Sit down by the fire, youngster, and rest yourself; for you'll have to go out with us again tonight, though not very far off."

Oliver did as he was told. He had not yet grasped that he was brought there to help them in the robbery; indeed, nothing had been said to him about the robbery.

He looked at Sikes in mute and timid wonder, and sat over the fire with an aching head in his hands; so tired out that he hardly knew what was passing round him.

The men at the table ate and drank, and Toby, half-filling a wineglass with spirits, ordered Oliver to drink it.

Oliver drank it in sheer fright, and immediately spluttered which delighted Toby Crackit and Barney, and even Sikes smiled.

After that the men stretched themselves on the chairs, and tried to sleep. Oliver fell into a heavy doze, when he was roused by Toby Crackit jumping up and declaring that it was half-past one.

Sikes and Toby put on their greatcoats, and buried their necks and chins in large dark shawls.

A pair of pistols were produced, which Toby stowed away. They also provided themselves with keys, a small crowbar, and other instruments for forcing locks, then the two robbers went into the black night with Oliver between them.

It was pitch dark, and very cold. They crossed the bridge, and soon arrived at the town of Chertsey.

They hurried through the main street of the little town, which at that late hour was quite deserted.

Then they turned up a road upon the left hand, and after walking about a quarter of a mile, they stopped before a detached house surrounded by a wall. Toby Crackit climbed the wall in a twinkling, and whispered to Sikes to hoist up the boy.

Sikes had him over in a trice, and the next moment climbed over himself. And then they all stole cautiously towards the house.

And now, for the first time, the terrified boy saw that house-breaking and robbery—perhaps murder—were the objects of the expedition. He gave a little cry of horror; the cold sweat stood upon his ashy face; his limbs failed him; and he fell.

"Get up," muttered Sikes, trembling with rage, and drawing the pistol from his pocket. "Get up, or I'll strew your brains upon the grass!"

"Oh! for God's sake, let me go!" cried Oliver. "Let me run away, and die in the fields! I will never come near London again;

never, never! Oh, pray, have mercy on me, and do not make me steal. For the love of God, have mercy on me!"

Sikes swore a dreadful oath, and had cocked his pistol, when Toby, striking it out of his grasp, placed his hand on the boy's mouth, and dragged him to the house, saying that the pistol shot would make a noise, and that—if it were necessary—he could easily finish Oliver with a crack on the head.

Sikes, vowing vengeance on Fagin for having sent a boy like Oliver on such an important piece of work, was now plying the crowbar deftly with very little noise, and with the assistance of Toby, the shutter swung open on its hinges.

It was a little lattice window, about five and a half feet from the ground, belonging to the scullery; the opening was very small—just big enough to admit a boy of Oliver's size. In a minute or two, Sikes, with the help of his tools, had the window open.

"Now listen, you young limb," whispered Sikes, drawing a dark lantern from his pocket, and throwing the glare full on Oliver's face; "I'm a-going to put you through there. Take this light; go softly up the steps straight afore you, and along the little hall to the street door; unfasten it, and let us in."

"There's a bolt at the top you won't be able to reach," put in Toby. "Stand upon one of the hall chairs. There are three there, Bill," added Toby, who for weeks past had been hanging round the place, finding out all he could—"three with a jolly large blue unicorn and gold pitchfork on 'em—which is the old lady's arms." And then he added, with a noiseless laugh, that Barney had enticed the dog away the night before.

Sikes lifted Oliver and put him gently through the window with his feet first, and, still holding on to his collar, planted him safely on the floor inside.

"Take this lantern," said Sikes, looking into the room. "You see the stairs afore you?"

Oliver, more dead than alive, gasped out, "Yes." Sikes pointed to the street door with the pistol barrel, and advised him to take notice that he was within shot all the way; and that if he faltered, he would fall dead that instant.

"What's that?" whispered Toby.

They listened intently.

"Nothing," said Sikes, releasing his hold of Oliver. "Now."

In the short time he had had to collect his senses, Oliver made up his mind that whether he died in the attempt or not, he would make one effort to dart up the stairs from the hall and alarm the family. Filled with this idea, he advanced stealthily.

"Come back!" suddenly cried Sikes, quite loud. "Back! Back!"

Oliver was so scared by the loud voice breaking on the stillness, and a loud cry that followed, that he let his lantern fall, and knew not whether to advance or to fly.

The cry was repeated; a light appeared; a vision of two terrified, half-dressed men at the top of the stairs swam before his eyes; a flash—a loud noise—a smoke—a crash somewhere—and Oliver staggered back.

Sikes had disappeared for an instant. But he was up again, and had Oliver by the collar before the smoke cleared away. He fired his own pistol after the men, who were already retreating; and dragged the boy up.

"Clasp your arm tighter," said Sikes, as he drew him through the window. "Give me a shawl here. They've hit him. Quick! How the boy bleeds!"

Then came the loud ringing of a bell, the noise of firearms, and the shouts of the men. Oliver felt himself being carried along

at a rapid pace. And then a cold deadly feeling crept over the boy's heart. Oliver had fainted.

The shouting of men rang through the air, and the barking of neighbouring dogs, roused by the sound of the alarm bell, resounded in every direction.

Sikes turned his head to look back at his pursuers; but there was little to be made out in the mist and darkness.

"Stop, you cowardly hound!" cried the robber, shouting after Toby Crackit, who, making the best use of his long legs, was already ahead. "Stop!"

Toby knew that he was not beyond the range of pistol-shot, and that Sikes was in no mood to be played with. And Toby came slowly back.

"Bear a hand with the boy!" cried Sikes furiously.

At this moment the noise grew louder. Sikes, again looking round, could see that the men, who had given chase, were already climbing the gate of the field in which he stood; and that a couple of dogs were some paces in advance of them.

"It's all up, Bill!" cried Toby. "Drop the kid, and show 'em your heels." And, with this parting advice, Mr. Crackit fairly turned tail, and darted off at full speed.

Sikes clenched his teeth; laid down the body of the wounded boy; threw over the helpless form of Oliver the cape in which he had been hurriedly muffled; ran along the front of the hedge, as if to take the attention of those behind from the spot where the boy lay, and whirling his pistol high into the air, he cleared the hedge at a bound, and was gone.

Three men, who had by this time advanced some distance into the field, stopped to take counsel together. The two first were the butler and footman of the lady whom Sikes had attempted

to rob; the third man was a travelling tinker, who had been sleeping in an outhouse that night, and had been roused by the other men to join in the pursuit.

They had been very brave up to this; but when they saw the burly form of the house-breaker bound over the hedge, whirling his pistol in the air, their blood suddenly cooled, and they stopped and turned back to the house.

Chapter Eight
At Mrs. Maylie's

The air grew colder as day came on. Oliver still lay motionless on the spot where Sikes had left him. Morning came, and with it rain. But Oliver, helpless and insensible, did not feel it.

At last, with a low cry of pain, the boy awoke. His left arm hung useless at his side, and the shawl in which it was wrapped was soaked with blood.

Wondering what the matter was, Oliver tried to rise; but he was trembling in every limb, and fell down like a log. Oliver made another effort, and, staggering and stumbling, moved slowly on, he knew not where.

He looked about and saw a house not very far off, and bent his faltering steps towards it, thinking that the people living there might have compassion on his wretched condition.

As he drew nearer, a feeling came over him that he had seen the place before. That garden wall! It was the very house they had attempted to rob!

Oliver was so much frightened when he remembered that, that he would have run away. Run! he could scarcely stand! And where, too, could he fly? He pushed the garden gate, which

Mr. Giles, looking at the pale faces round him, and very much afraid himself, suggested that somebody should open the door, and he looked at Brittles. Brittles did not answer, and the tinker had suddenly fallen asleep.

Then, after a little discussion, Mr. Giles hinted that they should go in a body to the door, to which suggestion they all immediately agreed, and the tinker woke up directly.

The cook and the housemaid, who were afraid to stay below, followed the men. And by the advice of Mr. Giles, they all talked very loud to warn the person outside that they were strong in numbers. Mr. Giles also suggested that the dogs' tails should be well pinched, in the hall, to make them bark savagely.

Brittles got well behind the door before he opened it at Mr. Giles's command; and the timid group, peeping over each other's shoulders, saw—looking up with piteous eyes, too exhausted to speak—a poor little wounded boy, almost unconscious from pain.

The whole company grew wonderfully brave, and Mr. Giles immediately dragged Oliver into the hall, Brittles and he recognizing him in a moment as the house-breaker they had shot.

"Here's one of the thieves, ma'am!" shouted Giles up the stairs. "Here's a thief, miss! Wounded, miss! I shot him, miss; and Brittles held the light!"

And the cook and the housemaid rushed upstairs to repeat that Giles had captured one of the robbers.

In the midst of all this confusion, a sweet voice was heard calling, "Giles?" and the servants stopped talking all at once.

"Hush!" said the voice, which belonged to the niece of the old lady; "you frighten my aunt as much as the thieves did. Is the poor creature much hurt?"

"Wounded desperate, miss," replied Giles, with the greatest satisfaction.

"Wait quietly one instant," said the young lady, "while I speak to my aunt."

She tripped softly away, and soon returned with the direction that the wounded house-breaker was to be carried carefully to Giles's room; and Brittles was to ride to Chertsey for a doctor and a constable.

"But won't you look at him first, miss?" asked Giles, with as much pride as if Oliver were some bird of rare plumage that he had skilfully brought down. "Not one little peep, miss?"

"Not now, for the world," replied the young lady. "Poor fellow! Oh! treat him kindly, Giles, for my sake!"

Oliver was carried upstairs, and by-and-by the doctor arrived. He was upstairs a long time with Oliver.

At last Dr. Losberne came down.

"This is a very extraordinary thing, Mrs. Maylie," said he. "Have you seen this thief?"

"No," rejoined the old lady.

Now Giles was so proud at his having shot a thief, that he had not as yet made up his mind to let his mistress know that it was only a little boy.

"Rose wished to see the man," said Mrs. Maylie, "but I would not hear of it."

"Humph!" rejoined the doctor. "There's nothing very alarming in his appearance. Have you any objection to see him in my presence?"

"Certainly not," replied the old lady, "if it be necessary."

They had expected to see a dogged, black-visaged ruffian in the burglar whom Giles had shot. And lo! there lay on the bed a

mere child, worn with pain and weakness, and sunk into a deep sleep. His wounded arm, bound and splintered up, was crossed in his breast; his head reclined on the other arm.

"What can this mean?" exclaimed the old lady. "This poor child can never have been the pupil of robbers?"

The doctor hinted that it was only too likely.

"But at so early an age!" urged Rose.

"Crime is not confined to the old alone," the doctor replied.

"But even if he has been wicked," went on Rose, "think how young he is. Ill-usage and blows, or the want of bread, may have driven him to join with men who have forced him to guilt."

And then, in a burst of agitation, Rose implored her aunt to have mercy on the wretched boy.

"My dear love," said the old lady, "do you think I would harm a hair of his head? My days are drawing to their close; and may mercy be shown to me as I show it to others." And then she asked the doctor what they could do to screen the boy, for a constable was already downstairs.

After a good deal of discussion, they came to the conclusion that they would do nothing till the boy awoke, and could give some account of himself.

The doctor went downstairs to tell the constable that, for the present, Oliver could not be moved or spoken to.

Hour after hour went by; and Oliver still slumbered. It was evening when the doctor brought the news that the child was sufficiently restored to be spoken to. The boy was very ill and weak from loss of blood; but his mind was so troubled from anxiety to disclose something, that he thought it best to let him do so.

Then the ladies accompanied him into the room; and, bit by bit, Oliver told them all his simple history. It was a solemn thing

to hear, in the darkened room—the feeble voice of the child recounting a list of evils which hard men had brought upon him.

Even the doctor was obliged to wipe his eyes at the end of Oliver's story. And then he went downstairs to bully Giles and Brittles into thinking that Oliver was not the boy they had shot.

"Tell me this," said Dr. Losberne, after he had frightened them enough, "tell me this, both of you! Are you going to take upon yourselves to swear that the boy upstairs is the boy that was put through the little window last night? Out with it! Come! We are prepared for you!"

The doctor, who was generally considered one of the best-tempered men on earth, looked so angry, that Giles and Brittles, who were considerably muddled by ale and excitement, stared at each other in a stupid way.

"Pay attention to the reply, constable, will you?" said the doctor solemnly. "Here's a house broken into, and a couple of men catch one moment's glimpse of a boy, in the midst of gunpowder and smoke. Here's a boy comes to the very same house next morning, and because he happens to have his arm tied up, these men lay violent hands upon him, and swear he is the thief."

Giles and Brittles looked doubtfully at each other, and then the bell rang violently, and Brittles announced, with some awe, that the Bow Street officers, whom Giles had sent for in the morning, had arrived to carry the captured robber off to prison.

The good doctor was rather taken aback at that, and to gain time he was a very long while explaining how the robbery had been attempted to the newly arrived men, who were named Blathers and Duff.

"Now, what is this about this here boy that the servants are a-talking on?" said Blathers.

"Nothing at all," replied the doctor. "One of the frightened servants chose to take it into his head that he had something to do with the robbery. But it's nonsense—sheer absurdity."

"Who is the boy?" asked Blathers, playing with a pair of handcuffs. "Where did he come from? He didn't drop out of the clouds, did he, master?"

"Of course not," replied the doctor, with a nervous glance at the two ladies, who had come to see the constables. "I know his whole history; but we can talk of that presently. You would like first to see the place where the thieves made their attempt, I suppose?"

"Certainly," rejoined Blathers. "We had better inspect the premises first, and examine the servants afterwards. That's the usual way of doing business."

Lights were then procured, and all the servants conducted Blathers and Duff to the little window through which Sikes had put Oliver.

After that had been thoroughly examined from inside and outside too, they were provided with a lantern to trace the footsteps with, and after that they were given a pitchfork to poke the bushes.

Then the two men had a long consultation about the matter by themselves.

All this time Dr. Losberne was walking up and down very uneasily, Mrs. Maylie and Rose watching him anxiously.

"Upon my word, I hardly know what to do," said the doctor.

They were all very much put about that Giles had sent for these Bow Street officers. Without them the doctor felt that he could easily have bullied Giles and Brittles into acknowledging that they had made a mistake in imagining Oliver was the boy they had shot.

Rose suggested that Oliver's story should be told to the men, as he had told it to them. But the doctor shook his head. He said he was probably an old fool for believing Oliver's story; but believe it he did. All the same, he did not think it was a tale that these practised police officers would believe.

"The more I think of it," said the kind-hearted old man, "the more I see that it will occasion endless trouble and difficulty if we tell these men the boy's real story. I am certain it will not be believed. And even if they do nothing to him in the end, still, the dragging it forward must interfere with your kind plan for rescuing him from misery."

While they were still talking, there came a knock at the door, and Blathers and Duff entered.

They were agreed, they said, that the robbery had been attempted by two persons, who certainly had a boy with them, small enough to squeeze through the window. And then they asked to see the lad.

The doctor immediately suggested, looking at Mrs. Maylie, that they should have something to drink first.

Rose went to the sideboard very willingly, and the doctor, satisfying himself that the men were about to enjoy themselves, slipped upstairs to his patient.

By-and-by he came down again, and asked the constables to step up to Oliver's room, into which Giles led them with a candle.

Oliver was half asleep and very feverish. The doctor helped him to sit up, but the boy was too ill to be conscious of what was going on around him.

"This," said Dr. Losberne, "is the lad, who, being accidentally wounded by a spring gun in some boyish trespass on Mr. What-d'ye-call-him's grounds, at the back here, comes to the house

for assistance this morning, and is immediately laid hold of by that clever gentleman with the candle in his hand, who has placed this boy's life in considerable danger."

Blathers and Duff looked at Giles, and Giles looked perplexed.

"You don't mean to deny that, I suppose?" said the doctor, laying Oliver gently down again.

"I'm sure I thought it was the boy," said the frightened Giles, "or I wouldn't have meddled with him."

And when Blathers questioned him, the poor old butler became more and more confused, and at last said he could not swear to him, and did not think it was the same boy, indeed.

Then the constables went down and questioned Brittles, who was just as confused as Giles, and, in the end, the police officers took themselves off.

Oliver gradually grew better. How he longed to get strong and well, to do something to show his gratitude to the gentle ladies who had taken care of him!

Oliver spoke of Mr. Brownlow, and of the good old housekeeper who had been so kind to him, and said how he longed to see them again, and let them know that he had repaid them ill—as it must seem to them—for all their goodness to him.

Rose said that they, too, had been thinking of that, and Dr. Losberne had promised to take him to London to see Mr. Brownlow, as soon as he could bear the journey.

Poor Oliver could have cried for joy. But alas! when that happy day came round at last, and he was able to go with the doctor to London, they found Mr. Brownlow's house empty, with a notice in the window "To Let."

They asked next door if the people could tell where Mr. Brownlow had moved, and they were told that Mr. Brownlow

and a friend of his, and the housekeeper too, had left England for the West Indies six weeks ago.

It was a terrible disappointment.

Oliver, who had never dreamed for a moment of not finding them, was miserably dejected; and the idea that they had gone away with the belief that he was an impostor and a thief was almost more than he could bear.

Chapter Nine
Fagin's Secret

And now we must go back to Fagin for a bit, and to the old den where Oliver had spent such lonely days.

Fagin was brooding over a dull, smoky fire. He was thinking deeply with his eyes fixed thoughtfully on the rusty bars.

Behind him at a table sat the Dodger and Charley Bates; they were playing cards with another member of the gang, Tom Chitling—who had just been released from prison.

Fagin took no notice of them, for he was buried in his thoughts, which were far from happy ones. Though he had not set eyes on Sikes or Toby Crackit since Sikes's departure from London with Oliver, he knew quite well that the robbery they had attempted at Chertsey had failed.

In his pocket was a newspaper with a full account of the attempted burglary and its miserable failure; and Fagin cursed their bad luck over and over again.

Where was Sikes? Where was Toby Crackit? In hiding, of course, he knew. And Oliver? He grew restless as he thought of Oliver; and he wished with all his heart he had the boy back.

Just then, the street bell tinkled softly.

The Dodger crept upstairs with the light, and returning, after a pause, whispered mysteriously to Fagin.

"What?" cried Fagin, "alone?"

The Dodger nodded.

"Where is he?" he asked.

The Dodger pointed to the chamber above. Fagin told him to bring him down.

The man who followed the Dodger was dressed in a coarse smock-frock, and had the lower portion of his face hidden in a large wrapper, which he pulled off now, and disclosed—all haggard, and unshorn—the features of Flash Toby Crackit.

"How are you, Faguey?" he asked in an off-hand way. But he looked as if he had bad news, and dreaded giving it.

Fagin motioned to the Dodger to put food on the table, and waited as patiently as he could while Toby ate. Then he ordered the Dodger out of the room, "First and foremost, Faguey, how is Bill?" asked Toby.

"What?" screamed Fagin, starting from his seat.

"Why, you don't mean to say?. . ." began Toby, turning pale.

"Mean!" cried Fagin, stamping furiously on the ground. "Where are they? Sikes and the boy? Where have they been? Where are they hiding? Why have they not been here?"

"The crack failed." said Toby faintly.

"I know it," cried Fagin, tearing the newspaper from his pocket. "What more?"

"They fired and hit the boy. We cut over the fields, with him between us through hedge and ditch. They gave chase. Curse me! the whole country was awake, and the dogs upon us."

"The boy?" screamed Fagin.

"Bill had him on his back, and scudded like the wind. We

stopped to take him between us; his head hung down, and he was cold. They were close upon our heels;—every man for himself, and each one from the gallows! We parted company, and left the youngster lying in a ditch. Alive or dead, that's all I know."

Fagin stopped to hear no more. But, uttering a loud yell, and twining his hands in his hair, he rushed from the house.

Now the other members of the gang believed, without thinking very much about it, that Fagin's anxiety to keep Oliver with him, and make him a thief, was merely to keep him quiet, and prevent him from telling tales, should he ever escape again.

But the wily old man had a deeper design than that—a secret that none of the others even guessed. He had learned, by the merest chance, the true story of Oliver's birth, from a man who had seen and recognized the boy from his likeness to his mother, the first day that Oliver had accompanied the Dodger and Charley Bates on their pickpocketing expedition.

This man, who called himself Monks, had sought out Fagin, and learned, to his consternation, that Oliver had been befriended by Mr. Brownlow. He then struck a bargain with Fagin, that if Oliver was got back, Fagin should have a large sum of money if he should make Oliver a thief.

Learning, too, from Fagin, the name of the workhouse where Oliver was born, the stranger had found his way there, and—by bribing this one and questioning that one—he had secured at last a little gold locket with the name "Agnes" engraved on the inside, which the old pauper woman, who had nursed Oliver's young mother, had stolen from her dead body.

This was positive proof to Monks that Oliver was the child he wanted; and hearing later on that Fagin had kidnapped Oliver from Mr. Brownlow's, he became desperate in his anxiety that

Oliver should be made a thief, bribing the old man with larger and larger sums.

It was not likely that such a wary old villain as Fagin was going to do Monks's work blindfold. Not he. He would learn the reason why, so that he might have a hold over Monks as well.

So he learned that little Oliver was Monks's half-brother; and that, in their father's will, the greater part of his money was left to *Agnes*, the mother of the younger boy, and, failing her, to her child; but only on the condition that *in his youth he should never have stained his name with any public act of dishonour, meanness, or wrong*. If the money failed to come to Oliver, Monks would have it all.

This, then, was Monks's object in trying to make the boy a thief. And Fagin's object was greed—the large sums offered him by Monks, if he, Fagin, should succeed in making Oliver steal.

No wonder, then, that Fagin uttered a yell of despair at Toby Crackit's story, as he rushed out of the house. And found his way to a low public-house called The Three Cripples. It was the meeting-place of thieves and bad characters.

The inn was full of people; and Fagin, catching the eye of the landlord, beckoned him out.

"Is *he* here?" he asked.

The man answered, "No."

"Will *he* be here tonight?" asked Fagin.

"Monks, do you mean?" inquired the landlord

"Hush! Yes."

"Certain," replied the man, drawing a gold watch from his pocket. "I expected him here before now. If you'll wait…"

"No, no," said Fagin hastily. "Tell him I came here to see him, and that he must now come to me. Tomorrow will be time enough."

He went down the street again, his face working with anxiety, and found his way to Sikes's house, to question Nancy.

Nancy had heard nothing of Bill. She looked very ill herself; and Fagin, trying to rouse her, said, "And the boy, too. Poor little child! Left in a ditch, Nance—only think!"

"The child is better where he is than among us," cried Nancy passionately. "And if no harm comes to Bill, I hope Oliver lies dead in the ditch."

"What!" cried Fagin.

"Ay, I do," returned the girl. "The sight of him turns me against myself and all of you."

This made Fagin very angry. He said, threateningly, that if Bill came home without Oliver, dead or alive, Nancy had better murder Bill, or he, Fagin, would himself kill Sikes.

"What's all this?" cried Nancy, surprised at his working face.

"What is it?" said Fagin, mad with rage, "when the boy's worth hundreds of pounds to me?. . ."

He stammered and caught himself up quickly, and looked frightened and guilty, staring at Nancy slily, to see if she had taken in what he had said in his mad rage.

"Did you mind me, Nancy dear?" he croaked softly.

Nancy had heard quite well, but she was cunning, too. Had she not been his pupil, indeed?

"Don't worry me now, Fagin," she said. "I'm too stupid to listen. If there's anything you want me to do, you had better wait till tomorrow." She resumed her listless air. And the Fagin's further remarks could not rouse her in the least.

He went off by-and-by quite satisfied that she had not taken in what he had let out; and a piercing wind drove him—trembling and shivering—homewards. He had just reached his own door,

and was fumbling for the key, when a dark figure crossed the road and glided up to him.

"Fagin!" whispered a voice close to his ear.

"Ah!" he said, turning quickly round, "is that…?"

"Yes," interrupted the stranger. "I have been lingering here these two hours. Where have you been?"

It was Monks. And he asked for news now, with a sneer.

"Nothing good," said Fagin.

"Nothing bad, I hope?" said Monks, with a startled look at him.

Then they both went in; and held a long whispered conversation about the robbery, and Oliver's having been left in the ditch.

Monks was fearfully excited. He was afraid that the boy had escaped him after all.

"I tell you it was badly planned," said he. "Why not have kept the boy here among the rest, and made a sneaking pickpocket of him at once? You've done it with others, scores of times."

"It was not easy to train him to the business," answered Fagin. "He was not like other boys in the same circumstances. We had enough of it, sending him out with the Dodger and Charley."

"That was not my doing," observed Monks.

"No, no," replied Fagin. "But we got him back by means of Nancy. And since then she has favoured him."

"Throttle the girl!" said Monks impatiently.

"Well, we can't afford to do that just now, my dear," returned Fagin, smiling. "But you want to make the boy a thief. Well, if he's alive, I can make him one from this time. But if the worst comes to the worst, and he is dead…"

"It's no fault of mine, if he is!" interrupted Monks, with a look of terror; and he clasped Fagin's arm with trembling hands. "Mind that, Fagin! I had no hand in it. Anything but his death—

I told you from the first. I won't shed blood. It's always found
out, and, besides, it haunts a man... What's that?"

"What?" cried Fagin, grasping the coward round the body with
both arms, as he sprang to his feet. "Where?"

"Yonder!" replied the man, glaring at the opposite wall. "The
shadow! I saw the shadow of a woman, in a cloak and bonnet,
pass along the wainscot like a breath!"

They rushed from the room. The candle had been standing
just where it had been placed. It showed them only the empty
staircase, and their own white faces.

"It's your fancy," said Fagin.

"I'll swear I saw it!" replied Monks, trembling. "It was bending forward when I saw it first; and when I spoke, it darted away."

They looked into all the rooms, and searched the passage outside. But they found nothing.

It was not fancy, however, though they did not know that till a
long time afterwards. The cunning Nancy had followed Fagin,
and had heard their conversation.

Chapter Ten
The Face at the Window

Meanwhile, Oliver, at the country cottage, with Mrs. Maylie
and her niece, was having a happy time.

The days were peaceful and quiet. The nights brought with them
neither fear nor care.

Every morning he went to an old gentleman that lived near
the little church, who taught him to read better, and to write;
and who spoke so kindly, and took such pains, that Oliver felt he
could never please him enough.

The spring flew swiftly by, and summer came, and the same quiet life went on at the little cottage, till one sad night when Rose was struck down by a fever.

She was very ill. Mrs. Maylie never left the bedside of her niece, and Oliver stole about the house in fear and trembling. Dr. Losberne muttered thickly that there was very little hope; and he used the utmost of his skill to ease the suffering girl.

At last she fell into a deep sleep from which she would awaken, the doctor said, "either to recovery and life, or to bid them farewell and die."

They sat listening, and afraid to speak for hours. The untasted meal was removed, and they watched the sun sink lower and lower, till dusk and dark came on. Their quick ears heard at last the doctor's step, and they ran to the door to meet him, Mrs. Maylie imploring him in the name of Heaven to tell her all.

"As God is good and merciful," the doctor said, almost weeping himself, "she will live to bless us all for years to come."

Then Harry Maylie, the old lady's son, arrived to hear the blessed news. And everyone could plainly see that he was in love with Rose.

By-and-by the daily routine of the house went on again, and with it Oliver's lessons. The little room in which he used to prepare them looked into a garden, whence a wicket gate opened into a small paddock, and beyond that was wood and meadow land.

One evening, just before twilight came, Oliver sat at this window preparing his lessons for the next morning. It had been a very hot day, and, as he had been running about a good deal, he was tired, and he gradually fell asleep. Then, as if in a dream, he thought, with a pang of terror, that he was in the Fagin's den

again. There sat the hideous old man, pointing at him, and whispering to another man, who sat beside him.

"Hush, my dear," he thought he heard him say, "it is he sure enough. Come away."

"He!" the other man seemed to answer, "could I mistake him, think you? If a crowd of ghosts were to put themselves into his exact shape, and he stood amongst them, there is something that would tell me how to point him out."

The man seemed to say this with such dreadful hatred, that Oliver awoke, and started up in fear.

Good Heaven! what was that! There—there—at the window close before him, with his eyes peering into the room, and meeting his—there stood Fagin. And beside him, white with rage, the scowling features of the very man whom he had pushed against in the village—Monks!

It was but an instant—a flash before his eyes; and they were gone. But they had recognized him, and he them. He stood transfixed for a moment; then he loudly cried for help, shouting, "Fagin! Fagin!"

In a moment, Harry Maylie, who had heard Oliver's story from his mother, with Dr. Losberne and Giles, was speeding towards the wood in search of the men. But all in vain. They could not find a glimpse of them.

"It must have been a dream, Oliver," said Harry Maylie.

"Oh, no, indeed, sir!" replied the boy, with a shudder. "I saw him too plainly for that.

"Who was the other?" inquired Harry.

"The very same man I told you of, who came so suddenly upon me at the inn. We had our eyes fixed full upon each other. He leaped over just there; and Fagin crept through that gap."

And Oliver's face looked too earnest for the two gentlemen to doubt the truth of his words.

"This is strange!" said Harry Maylie.

On the next day fresh search was made, but with no better success; and, inquire as they would, their efforts to discover Fagin and his companion were altogether fruitless.

A few days after that, Harry Maylie went away, and when Rose was recovered, the family went for a time to London.

And while they are stopping at a hotel near Hyde Park, we must go back for a bit to Nancy.

Chapter Eleven
Nancy

The conversation she had heard between Monks and Fagin haunted Nancy. She had heard just enough to know that they were very anxious to get Oliver into their hands again, for some bad purpose of Monks; but not enough to know what that purpose was. Monks had spoken with such hatred of Oliver, that the girl trembled to think of Fagin's ever getting hold of the boy again, and wished with all her heart that the child were dead, rather than that he should be captured again.

His little, innocent, frightened face would not let her rest, and it troubled her conscience often. And now that he had got away once more, she hoped that they would never set eyes on him again. She would rather know that he was dead.

Sikes had found his way to London after living in hiding for a while; but he had come home very ill. Those long tramps in the rain had given him a chill, which had brought on a fever at last.

But Nancy nursed him through it all. And Sikes, still weak and

ill, was able to sit up at last; Then Fagin, hearing of his recovery, thought it high time to make amends for any neglect of the past few weeks.

"What evil wind has blowed you here?" growled Sikes, whose temper had not been improved by illness.

"No evil wind at all, my dear; for evil winds blow nobody any good. And I've brought something good with me, that you'll be glad to see." And then Fagin told the Dodger, who had accompanied him, with Charley Bates, to open the bundle, and let Bill see the good things they had brought for him.

The Dodger immediately did so, and produced a rabbit pie, and half-a-pound of tea; some sugar, a pat of butter, a piece of cheese, and a full bottle of spirits, which Charley Bates uncorked.

"Well, what have you to say for yourself," went on Sikes.

Fagin begged him not to be cross. And, after a little more squabbling, Sikes demanded some money.

"Well, well," said Fagin, with a sigh, "I'll send the Artful round."

"You won't do nothing of the kind," rejoined Mr. Sikes. "The Artful's a deal too artful, and would forget to come, or lose his way, or anything, if you put him up to it. Nancy shall go and fetch it, to make all sure. Five pounds no less!"

After a good deal of haggling, Fagin beat him down to three pounds four-and-sixpence. And Sikes sullenly agreed, on condition that Nancy was to return with Fagin that night to fetch it. So Fagin, the boys and Nancy got up to go.

They found Toby Crackit playing cards with Tom Chitling in the old den. Fagin ordered Tom and the boys off on a pickpocketing expedition.

"Now," said Fagin, when they had left the room, "I'll go and get you that cash, Nancy." But while he was speaking the bell

that
such s
Then M
to bring dow
through every j
for some dreadful

tinkled, and presently the visitor was ushered downstairs. Nancy had never seen him before, and did not know who he was, but she remembered the voice—the voice of the man who had spoken with such hatred of Oliver.

He said he had had good news, and asked for a word with Fagin, and he looked suspiciously at Nancy. Nancy threw him a careless glance, as if he did not interest her at all, and then looked away.

Fagin said he would not keep her waiting ten minutes, and took his visitor into an upstairs room. In a moment the girl slipped off her shoes, and, gliding from the room, ascended the stairs softly and silently.

Listening intently, she gleaned from their conversation that they had found out where Oliver was, the visitor saying that Heaven had gone against him in putting Oliver into the hands of Mrs. Maylie, who, he was sure, would give hundreds and thousands of pounds, if she had them, to know who Oliver was. He told Fagin he had found out that the Maylies were in London, with Oliver, and mentioned the name of the hotel where they were staying, near Hyde Park.

And he added, with dreadful oaths and expressions of hatred, that if the boy took advantage of his birth and history, he might harm even the speaker himself.

"In short, Fagin," the visitor continued—for he was no other n Monks—"Crooked as you are, you never laid for anyone ares as I'll contrive to lay for my young brother Oliver." onks, getting very wild, said what a game it would be n the boast of the father's will, by driving Oliver ail in the town, and getting him hauled up at last crime.

Nancy stole down, trembling and pale.

So white was she that Fagin—having seen Monks off the premises—started back as he entered the room. "Why, Nance," he said, "how pale you are! What have you been doing?"

Nancy said, as carelessly as she could, that the place was stuffy and close, and urging him to let her have the money, bade him goodnight, and hurried off as soon as she got it.

She gave the money to Sikes who then fell into a deep sleep. Nancy had made up her mind to let the Maylies know the danger that threatened Oliver.

She put on her bonnet and shawl, and hurrying along, Set off towards the West End. As she reached the hotel that Monks had mentioned to Fagin, the clock struck eleven.

It was with some difficulty that Nancy got the porter to take up a message to Miss Maylie, but the man consented, and came down to tell the trembling Nancy she was to walk upstairs.

Rose received her alone, and spoke so gently, and asked so kindly what she could do for her, that Nancy burst into tears.

"Oh, lady, lady!" she said, clasping her hands passionately, "if there was more like you, there would be fewer like me."

"Sit down," said Rose earnestly. "If you are in poverty or trouble, I shall be truly glad to relieve you, if I can."

"Let me stand," said the girl, "Is—is that door shut?"

"Yes," said Rose, recoiling a few steps. "Why?"

"Because I am about to put my life, and the lives of others, into your hands. I am the girl that dragged little Oliver back to old Fagin's, on the night he went out from the house in Pentonville," sobbed Nancy. And then she whispered low—"Do you know a man named Monks?"

Rose said she had never heard the name. And Nancy, very

much agitated, told her of the two conversations she had heard between Fagin and Monks concerning Oliver.

"You don't mean," said Rose, turning very pale, "that this was said in earnest?"

"He spoke in hard, angry earnest, if a man ever did," replied Nancy, shaking her head. "He is an earnest man when his hatred is up." And then she added that she must go.

Rose then begged her to stay—promising her that she would help her to live a better life.

But Nancy shook her head decidedly; though she wept too, saying, "It was too late!—Too late!" and though they were desperate characters, her life was bound up with theirs.

"But what am I to do?" asked Rose. "This mystery must be looked into, or how will your telling it to me benefit Oliver?"

"You must have some kind gentleman about you that will hear it as a secret," Nancy said, "and advise you what to do."

"But where can I find you again?" asked Rose.

Then Nancy made her promise that her secret should be strictly kept, and that she should not be watched or followed if she agreed to meet Rose and a gentleman later on.

Rose promised solemnly. And Nancy said that she would walk on London Bridge every Sunday night from eleven till twelve.

Chapter Twelve
Oliver Sees Mr. Brownlow

Rose said nothing of the strange visit to Mrs. Maylie that night, fearing that her first impulse would be to confide in Doctor Losberne, for Rose was too well acquainted with the good doctor's hasty temper to trust him with such a secret.

At last she thought she would write to Harry Maylie; and the next morning she was just going to begin her letter, when Oliver, who had been walking about the streets, with Giles for a body-guard, rushed back to the hotel in a great state of excitement, with the news that he had seen Mr. Brownlow getting out of a coach, and going into a house.

"I didn't speak to him. I couldn't speak to him, for he didn't see me. But Giles asked for me if he lived there, and they said he did. Look here," said Oliver, opening a scrap of paper, "here it is. Here's where he lives. I'm going there directly! Oh! what shall I do when I come to see him, and hear him speak again!"

"Quick!" said Rose. "Tell them to fetch a coach. I will take you there myself—directly." Surely Mr. Brownlow would be the one to help her in her difficulty, she thought, with a glad feeling of relief—Mr. Brownlow, who had been so much interested in Oliver. She made up her mind to tell Mr. Brownlow Nancy's story; and waited impatiently to set off.

The coach was procured, and away they went, the child hardly able to contain himself in his excitement.

Rose made Oliver stay in the coach, while she sent up her card, asking if she could see Mr. Brownlow on a little business.

And in another moment Rose was conducted in, where she found Mr. Brownlow sitting with his old friend, Mr. Grimwig.

She had no sooner mentioned the name Oliver Twist, than Mr. Grimwig dropped his book in his astonishment, and fell back into his chair. Mr. Brownlow drew his seat nearer to Miss Maylie's, and begged her, in Heaven's name, to tell him what she knew of Oliver's character.

Rose coloured as she began to relate in a few words all that had befallen Oliver since he left Mr. Brownlow's house.

"Thank God!" cried the old gentleman. "This is great happiness to me." And he rushed out to the coach to bring Oliver in.

"Send Mrs. Bedwin here, if you please," cried Mr. Brownlow, as he came in with Oliver.

"God be good to me!" cried the old housekeeper. "It is my innocent boy!"

"My dear old nurse," cried Oliver, springing into her arms; while the good soul laughed and wept upon his neck in turns.

And leaving her with Oliver, Mr. Brownlow led Rose into another room, where she gave him a full account of her strange interview with Nancy.

The old gentleman considered that she had acted prudently in not confiding the matter to such a hasty man as the doctor, and agreed that Nancy's confidence should not be betrayed, telling her to break the news cautiously to Mrs. Maylie, and that when the doctor came to London, he would tell him the tale.

Chapter Thirteen
An Old Enemy

In the meantime, who in the world should come tramping up to London but Oliver's old enemy—Noah Claypole, accompanied by Mrs. Sowerberry's servant, Charlotte!

They had robbed the undertaker, and run off.

Noah made his way, and stopped, by the merest chance, at the public-house used by Fagin and his gang—The Three Cripples.

Fagin appeared, to make inquiries after some of his young pupils and he was informed in a whisper of the suspicious-looking country pair; and Fagin's ear was at the peephole in a trice.

Fagin listened attentively, and, from the conversation which

he overheard, he soon learned that the worthy pair had robbed a till and had got away with the money.

This was after Fagin's own heart. He rubbed his dirty hands together, and by-and-by entered the room with a low bow, and a very amiable smile; and sitting himself down at the nearest table, he ordered something to drink.

"A pleasant night, sir, but cool for the time of year," said Fagin. "From the country I see, sir."

"How do yer see that?" asked Noah Claypole.

"We have not so much dust as that in London," replied Fagin, pointing from Noah's shoes to those of Charlotte.

It was an easy matter for the wily old man to enter into further talk with Noah, and then gradually to let him know that he had learned his secret.

Noah was very much frightened at first, and blamed Charlotte.

"I didn't take it," he stammered. "It was all her doing. Yer've got it now, Charlotte, yer know yer have."

"No matter who's got it, or who did it, my dear," replied Fagin. "I'm in that way myself, and I like you for it."

"In what way?" asked Mr. Claypole, a little recovering.

"In that way of business," rejoined Fagin, "and so are the people of the house. You've hit the right nail upon the head, and are as safe here as you could be."

After a little more talk, Noah ordered Charlotte out of the room, while he and Fagin held a whispered conversation on the advisability of Noah's joining Fagin's gang.

After that, the matter was settled very amicably, on the condition that Noah then and there should hand over to Fagin the twenty-pound note that Charlotte had stolen.

Noah made a wry face at that. But there was no help for it,

Fagin hinting that he was doing a favour in employing him at all, which he would not have dreamed of doing, if he had not been rather short of assistants at that moment.

So the bargain was made, and they parted for the night, on the understanding that Noah was to find his way to Fagin's den next morning.

Fagin welcomed him heartily when he came; but he looked a little troubled. And then he informed Mr. Morris Bolter, sorrowfully, that his best hand was taken from him the day before.

"You don't mean to say he died!" cried Mr. Bolter.

"No, no," replied Fagin, "He was charged with attempting to pick a pocket, and they found a silver snuff-box on him."

No wonder the old man looked sad. It was quite true, indeed. The Dodger—the Artful Dodger—the cunning John Dawkins— had fallen into the hands of the police! A policeman had seen him take a handkerchief out of a gentleman's pocket, but finding it to be an old one, the Artful Dodger first blew his own nose in it and then returned it to the owner's pocket. The policeman kept his eye on him after that, and following him in the crowd, had taken him into custody. Then he was searched, and the silver snuff-box was discovered on his person.

"Transportation for life!" said Fagin sadly. "They'll make the Artful nothing less than a lifer."

While they were talking, Charley Bates walked in.

"It's all up, Fagin," he said. "They've found the gentleman as owns the box; two or three more's coming to 'dentify the Dodger. I must have a full suit of mourning, Fagin, and a hat-band, to visit him in, afore he sets out on his travels. To think of Jack Dawkins—lummy Jack—the Dodger—the Artful Dodger—going abroad for a common twopenny-halfpenny sneeze-box! I

never thought he'd a done it under a gold watch, chain, and seals, at the lowest. Oh, why didn't he rob some rich old gentleman of all his valuables, and go out as a gentleman.

After a little more talk, which turned chiefly on the cleverness of the Dodger, Fagin said that somebody must go to the police court to learn how the Dodger fared.

"Shall I go?" asked Charley.

"Not for the world," replied Fagin. "Are you mad, my dear?"

"Why don't you send Noah?" asked Master Bates. "Nobody knows him."

Noah consented after some hesitation.

Fagin dressed him up in a waggoner's frock, velveteen breeches, and leather leggings.

Charley Bates then led him through many winding ways to within a short distance of Bow Street, and promised to wait for him there till he returned.

And Noah, following the directions he had received, soon found himself in the police court amongst a lot of other spectators. He looked about for the Dodger; but could see no sign of him.

And then at last an individual—with big coatsleeves tucked half-way up his arms, his left hand deep in his pocket, and his hat in his right hand—came shuffling into the office immediately behind the jailer. And from the description given him by Charley, Noah knew that this was the famous Jack Dawkins.

"What's this?" asked one of the magistrates.

"A pickpocketing case, your worship."

"Has the boy ever been here before?"

"He ought to have been, a many times," replied the jailer. "He's been everywhere else. *I* know him well, your worship."

And then the clerk called for the witnesses. So a policeman

stepped up, to witness how he had seen the Dodger take a handkerchief from a gentleman's pocket, and blow his own nose in it
before putting it back; and how he had followed him till he got
near enough to take him into custody, when a silver snuff-box
was found on him. And then the gentleman that owned the snuff-
box came to witness that it was his, and that he had seen the
Dodger hanging about in the crowd.

"Have you anything to ask, boy?" asked the magistrate.

"I wouldn't abase myself to descending to hold no conwersation
with him." replied the Dodger.

"Have you nothing to say at all?"

The Dodger pretended not to hear, so the jailer nudged him,
and repeated what the magistrate had said.

The Dodger looked up as if roused from deep thinking. "I beg
your pardon,' he said, "did you redress yourself to me, my man?"

"I never see such an out-an-out young wagabond, your wor-
ships," said the jailer, with a grin. "Do you mean to say anything, you young shaver?"

"No," replied the Dodger, "not here, for this ain't the shop for
justice. Besides which, my attorney is a-breakfasting with the
Wice President of the House of Commons. But I shall have something to say elsewhere, and so will he, and so will a werry nu-
merous and 'spectable circle of acquaintance, as'll make them
beaks wish they'd never been born, or that they'd got their foot-
men to hang 'em up to their own hat-pegs, afore they'd let 'em
come out this morning to try it upon me. I'll …"

"There! He's fully commited!" said the clerk. "Take him away."

"Come on," said the jailer.

"Oh, ah! I'll come on," replied the Dodger, brushing his hat
with the palm of his hand. "Ah!" (to the magistrates) "it's no use

your looking frightened. I won't show you no mercy—not a ha'porth of it. *You'll* pay for this, my fine fellers. I wouldn't be you for something! I wouldn't go free now, if you was to fall down on your knees to ask me. Here, take me away!"

The jailer had him already by the collar of his coat, and was dragging him off, the Dodger threatening that he would make a "parliamentary business" of it, and then grinning in the jailer's face with great glee and self-approval.

But it was his last fling: and the Dodger knew it. He was locked up in a little cell by himself, and had plenty of time to ponder on the long journey before him, and a prisoner's life across the seas.

Noah went back to find Charley Bates, and the two hastened to Fagin's den, to tell him how the Artful Dodger had distinguished himself on his last appearance in public.

Chapter Fourteen
Noah Plays the Spy

Cunning though Nancy was, she could not help showing her restlessness. She remembered that both the crafty Fagin and the brutal Sikes had confided in her when they had hidden things from other members of the gang.

Much as she hated Fagin, she recoiled to think that he should fall at last by her hand, richly as he merited such a fate. But it comforted her to think that the beautiful lady had promised so solemnly to keep her secret; and that she, herself, had dropped no clue which could lead to the discovery of the gang.

But she was very wretched, and often sat silent and dejected, taking no part in the hilarious conversation where once she would have been the merriest.

The first Sunday night after her meeting with Rose, she tried to keep her appointment on London Bridge; but Sikes, though he was quite well now, was in a sullen mood, and wanted her to stay at home. When Nancy persisted in putting on her bonnet and shawl, Sikes got angry, and swore he would have his way, and taking her bonnet from her, flung it away.

"Tell him to let me go, Fagin," cried Nancy, turning to the old man, who was sitting in the room. "It'll be better for him. Do you hear me?"

Fagin looked thoughtful, but did not interfere, as Sikes flung her into a chair, and stood over her.

"Wot does it mean? Wot did she take it into her head to go out tonight for, do you think?" Bill asked him, as Nancy quieted down after a good deal of struggling and pleading.

"Woman's obstinacy, I suppose, my dear," said the old man.

"I suppose it is," growled Sikes. And then he added that Nancy had been shut up so long nursing him in his illness, that it had worried and fretted her.

"That's it, my dear," murmured Fagin. And he said goodbye. But he was thoughtful, very thoughtful, as he walked home. Nancy had been very strange lately—very moody and silent. And what did she want to go out for, so late, that Sunday night?

The old man, with a dark look, and a threatening motion of the hand, made up his mind that he would set one of the gang to spy on Nancy's movements. Bolter would do. Morris Bolter.

"Bolter," he said, drawing up a chair next morning, as Noah Claypole ate his breakfast, "Morris Bolter."

"Well, here I am," said Noah.

"I want you, Bolter," said Fagin, leaning over the table, "to do a piece of work for me, my dear, that needs great care."

"I say," rejoined Bolter, "don't yer go shoving me into danger, or sending me away to any more o' yer police offices. That don't suit me, that don't; and so I tell yer."

"There's not the smallest danger in it—not the very smallest," said Fagin. "It's only to dodge a woman."

"An old woman?" demanded Mr. Bolter.

"A young one," replied Fagin.

"I can do that pretty well, I know," said Bolter. "What am I to dodge her for?"

"Not to do anything," said Fagin, "but to tell me where she goes, who she sees, and, if possible, what she says."

"Who is she?" inquired Noah.

"One of us," answered Fagin.

"Oh, Lor'!" cried Noah, curling up his lip.

"She has found out some new friends, my dear, and I must know who they are," replied Fagin.

"I see," said Noah. "Just to have the pleasure of knowing them, if they're respectable people, eh? Ha! ha! ha! I'm your man."

"I knew you would be," answered Fagin.

"Where am I to wait for her? Where am I to go?"

"All that, my dear, you shall hear from me. I'll point her out at the proper time," said Fagin. "You keep ready."

Six nights passed. At last, on the seventh—Sunday—Fagin came in with an exultant face, and beckoned Noah out.

He took him to The Three Cripples, and made him look through the little pane of glass (through which Fagin himself had spied on Noah) at a woman who was sitting in the next room. It was Nancy. And Noah peeped till he had got her face by heart. "I should know her among a thousand," he said.

They waited till Nancy made a movement, and went out.

Noah then exchanged a look with Fagin, and darted noise-lessly after the girl. She looked nervously round two or three times, all unconscious of the spy behind her. But as she went, her courage came, and she made her way to London Bridge.

It was a very dark night; and the lady she had come to look for was nowhere to be seen. Nancy walked restlessly up and down; and the spy slunk at some distance, in the shadows.

At last, a hackney carriage drew up at a little distance from the Bridge; and a young lady, accompanied by a grey-haired gen-tleman, alighted, and walked towards the Bridge. They were Rose Maylie and Mr. Brownlow.

"You were not here last Sunday night," said Mr. Brownlow, who looked at her with pity.

"I couldn't come," replied Nancy.

After a little talk, Mr. Brownlow said he believed Nancy was to be trusted, and that he would confide to her, without reserve, that their aim was to secure Monks. But if Monks could not be secured, Nancy must deliver up Fagin.

"Fagin!" cried Nancy, recoiling. "Never!"

And she added firmly that, bad as he was, she would never give him up, because she had worked with him, and he had trusted her.

Then Mr. Brownlow said, "Put Monks into my hands, and leave him to me to deal with."

"What if he turns against the others?" Nancy asked

Mr. Brownlow said that their only object in wanting to secure Monks was to get at the bottom of his secret concerning Oliver; and if they got the truth from him, the others would go scotfree.

"Have I the lady's promise for that?" asked Nancy.

"You have," replied Rose. "My true and faithful pledge."

"Monks would never learn how you knew what you know now?" questioned the girl, after a pause.

"Never," said Mr. Brownlow. "The knowledge should be so brought to bear upon him, that he could never even guess."

"I have been a liar, and among liars from a little child," said Nancy, thinking a while, "but I will take your words."

They both promised her again to keep her secret. And Nancy—in such a low voice that the spy had to strain to listen—described to them the situation of The Three Cripples, and the night and hour on which Monks was most in the habit of frequenting it.

"He is tall," she said, "and has a lurking walk; and, as he walks, he constantly looks over his shoulder." She went on to describe his dark sunken-in eyes, and a broad red mark—like a burn or a scald—that he had upon his throat.

At that, Mr. Brownlow started, and muttered to himself, "It must be he." And then he told Nancy that she had given him valuable information, and asked what he could do to repay her.

"Nothing, sir," said Nancy, weeping.

And, weeping still, she implored them to leave her. Her agitation was so violent that Mr. Brownlow immediately drew Rose away.

And the spy darted away at his fullest speed, and made for the Fagin's den as fast as his legs could carry him.

Two hours later, Fagin, with face distorted and bloodshot eyes, sat crouching over a cold hearth, biting his long, black nails; and on a mattress, lay Noah Claypole fast asleep.

The old man sat without changing his attitude in the least. He was thinking—thinking deeply.

"At last," he muttered, Wiping his fevered mouth as his quick ear caught the sound of a footstep in the street.

The bell tinkled; and Fagin crept up the stairs to let in the burly form of Sikes.

"There!" said the robber, laying a bundle on the table. "Do the most you can with that. It's been enough trouble to get."

Fagin locked the bundle in the cupboard, and did not speak. And he looked at Sikes with his lips quivering so violently, and his face so altered by the emotions which mastered him, that the housebreaker drew back with a look of real fright.

"Wot now?" cried Sikes. "Wot do you look at a man so for?"

Fagin shook his trembling finger in the air, but his passion was so great that he could not speak for the moment.

"Speak, will you?" cried Sikes. "Open your mouth and say wot you've got to say in plain words. Out with it!"

"Suppose that lad," said Fagin, pointing to Noah, "was to peach—to blow upon us all, stealing out at nights."

"I'd grind his skull under the iron heel of my boot," muttered Sikes, with a terrible oath.

"If it was Charley, or the Dodger, or Bet, or…"

"I don't care who," replied Sikes impatiently; "whoever it was, I'd serve them the same."

Fagin looked hard at the robber. And then, stooping over the mattress on the floor, he roused Noah, who got up with a yawn.

"Tell that again—once again just for him to hear," urged Fagin.

"Tell yer what?" asked the sleepy Noah.

"That about—*Nancy*," said Fagin, clutching Sikes by the wrist. "You followed her?"

"Yes."

"To London Bridge?"

"Yes."

"Where she met two people?"

"So she did." And Noah went on to tell the conversation he had heard, the old man reminding him at the last to tell about the laudanum she had given Sikes.

With a fearful oath, the robber started up, and rushed violently from the room.

"Bill, Bill" cried Fagin, following him hastily.

"Let me out," cried Sikes. "Don't speak to me—it's not safe. Let me out, I say."

"You won't be too violent, Bill?"

Sikes made no reply; but pulling open the door, he dashed into the silent streets.

And the next morning all London rang with the news of a terrible crime. For Sikes had murdered Nancy.

Chapter Fifteen
The Fate of Sikes

Meanwhile, Mr. Brownlow, with the aid of a couple of men, immediately secured Monks, and had him taken in a carriage to his house.

Here he told Monks that he knew of all his villainy; that he knew too who he was, and why he had caused Oliver to be dragged back to Fagin's. And, addressing him as *Edward Leeford*, he asked him if he dared to brave him still.

It turned out then, that Mr. Brownlow had known Monks's father, who had been a dear friend of his; that he knew also of the will that left the greater part of his money to *Agnes*—Oliver's poor young mother—and after her to her child. Indeed, the picture of the beautiful lady that had so fascinated Oliver, when he was recovering under Mrs. Bedwin's care, was a likeness of

his own mother; but, at that time, Mr. Brownlow did not know, of course, that Oliver was her child.

When Monks learned how much Mr. Brownlow knew (for the old gentleman, in his anxiety, had even gone to the workhouse, and found out how Monks had bribed a woman there, and secured from her the locket that she had stolen from the dead body of Agnes), he gave in at once, and confessed the whole of his villainy; and promised to write down a true statement of the facts, if Mr. Brownlow would agree to settle the matter privately, and not bring the law to bear upon him.

The police surrounded The Three Cripples; and later on succeeded in pouncing on Fagin's den, and caught the old man before he could get away.

And where was Sikes?

Taking the dog with him, he had softly locked the door of the room where Nancy's body lay, and, taking the key, had left the house, and walked rapidly away.

He went through Islington; strode up the hill at Highgate, turned down to Highgate Hill, unsteady of purpose, and uncertain where to go.

He wandered over miles and miles of ground, and still came back to the old place.

Suddenly he took the desperate resolution of going back to London.

The dog, though! If any descriptions of Bull's-eye were out, it would not be forgotten that the dog was missing, and had probably gone with him. This might lead to Sikes's being taken as he passed along the streets. And Sikes determined to drown the dog.

He walked on, looking about for a pool; and picked up a heavy stone, and tied it in his handkerchief as he went.

The dog looked into his master's face, and something in the robber's look made him skulk behind. And when his master halted at the brink of a pool Bull's-eye stopped outright.

"Do you hear me call? Come here!" shouted Sikes.

The dog came up; but as Sikes stooped to tie the handkerchief to his throat, he uttered a low growl, and started away.

"Come back!" shouted the robber.

The dog wagged his tail, but moved not. Sikes made a running noose, and called him again.

The dog advanced—retreated—paused an instant—turned; then scoured away at his hardest speed.

Sikes whistled again and again, and sat down, and waited in the hope that the dog would soon return.

But no dog appeared, and he started on his journey once more.

In a low, dirty neighbourhood beyond Dockhead stands Jacob's Island, surrounded by a muddy ditch, six or eight feet deep, and fifteen or twenty feet wide when the tide is in, known, in the day of this story, as Folly Ditch—a creek or inlet from the Thames.

In Jacob's Island, the warehouses are roofless and empty; the walls are crumbling down; the doors are falling into the street. The houses have no owners; they are broken open, and entered upon by those who have the courage. They must be reduced to a destitute condition indeed who seek a refuge in Jacob's Island.

In an upper room of one of these houses—a detached house all falling to ruin, but strongly defended at door and window—there were assembled three men, eyeing each other in some perplexity, in a profound and gloomy silence.

One of these was Toby Crackit; another, Tom Chitling; and the third, a robber of fifty years, named Kags—an old member of Fagin's gang.

There was a short silence. Then Toby Crackit, giving up his swaggering air, turned to Chitling. "When was Fagin took?" he asked.

"Just at dinner-time—two o'clock this afternoon. Charley and I made our escape up the wash'us chimney, and Bolter got into the empty water-butt, head downwards; but his legs were so long that they stuck out at the top, and so they took him too."

"And Bet?"

"Poor Bet! She went to see the Body, to speak to who it was!" said Chitling, his countenance falling more and more—"and went off mad—screaming and raving, and beating her head against the boards! So they put a strait-weskit on her, and took her to the hospital; and there she is."

"Wot's come of young Bates?" demanded Kags.

"He hung about, not to come over here afore dark, but he'll be here soon," replied Chitling. "There's nowhere's else to go now, for the people at The Cripples are all in custody, and the bar of the den is filled with police."

"This *is* a smash," observed Toby, biting his lips. "There's more than one will go with this."

"The Sessions is on," said Kags. "If they get the inquest over, and Bolter turns King's evidence, as of course he will, from what he's said already, they can prove Fagin an accessory before the fact, and get the trial on on Friday, and he'll be hanged in six days from this."

Chitling got up and paced violently to and fro, like one distracted.

While he was thus engaged, and the two men sat by in silence, with their eyes fixed upon the floor, a pattering noise was heard upon the stairs, and Sikes's dog bounded into the room. They ran to the window downstairs, and into the street. The dog had

jumped in at an open window. He made no attempt to follow them, nor was his master to be seen.

"What's the meaning of this?" said Toby, when they had returned. "He can't be coming here. I—I—hope not."

"If he was coming here, he'd have come with the dog," said Kags, stooping down to examine the animal, who lay panting on the floor. "Here! Give us some water for him; he has run himself faint."

"He's drunk it all up, every drop," said Chitling, after watching the dog some time in silence. "Covered with mud—lame—half-blind—he must have come a long way!"

"Where can he have come from?" exclaimed Toby. "He's been to the other dens, of course, and finding them filled with strangers, he's come on here, where he's been many a time and often. But where can he have come from first? And how comes he here without the other?"

"He"—not one of them called the murderer by his name—"he can't have made away with hisself. What do you think?" said Chitling.

Toby shook his head.

"If he had," said Kags, "the dog 'ud want to lead us away to where he did it. No. I think he's got out of the country, and left the dog behind. He must have given him the slip somehow, or he wouldn't be so easy."

The dog, creeping under a chair, coiled himself up to sleep, without more notice from anybody.

It being now dark, the shutter was closed, and a candle lighted and placed upon the table. The terrible events of the last few days had made a deep impression on all three, increased by the danger and uncertainty of their own position.

They drew their chairs closer together, starting at every sound. They spoke little, and that in whispers, and were as silent and awe-stricken as if the remains of the murdered woman lay in the next room.

They had sat thus some time, when suddenly was heard a hurried knocking at the door below.

"Young Bates," said Kags, looking angrily round to check the fear he felt himself.

The knocking came again. No, it was not Bates. He never knocked like that.

Crackit went to the window, and—shaking all over—drew in his head. There was no need to tell them *who* it was. Toby's pale face was enough. The dog, too, was on the alert in an instant, and ran whining to the door.

"We must let him in," said Toby, taking up the candle.

"Isn't there any help for it?" asked the other man in a hoarse voice.

"None. He *must* come in."

"Don't leave us in the dark," said Kags, taking down a candle from the chimneypiece, and lighting it, with such a trembling hand, that the knocking was twice repeated before he had finished.

Crackit went down to the door, and returned, followed by a man with the lower part of his face buried in a handkerchief, and another tied over his head under his hat. He drew them slowly off. White face—sunken eyes—hollow cheeks—beard of three days' growth—wasted flesh—short thick breath! It was the very ghost of Sikes.

He laid his hand upon a chair which stood in the middle of the room, and—shuddering as he was about to drop into it, and

seeming to glance over his shoulder—dragged it back close to the wall, as close as it would go—ground it against it, and sat down.

Not a word had been exchanged. He looked from one to another in silence. If an eye were furtively raised and met his, it was instantly turned away. When his hollow voice broke the silence, they all three started. They seemed never to have heard its tones before.

"How came that dog here?" asked Sikes.

"Alone. Three hours ago."

"Tonight's paper says that Fagin's took. Is it true, or is it a lie?"

"True."

They were silent again.

"Curse you all!" said Sikes, passing his hand across his forehead. "Have you nothing to say to me?"

There was an uneasy movement among them, but nobody spoke.

"You that keep this house," said Sikes, turning his face to Crackit, "do you mean to sell me, or to let me lie here till this hunt is over?"

"You may stop here, if you think it safe," returned Crackit, after some hesitation.

Sikes carried his eyes slowly up the wall behind him; rather trying to turn his head than actually doing it. Said he, "Is it—the—the body—is it buried?"

They shook their heads.

"Why isn't it?" he retorted, with the same glance behind him. "Wot do they keep such ugly things above the ground for? Who's that knocking?"

Crackit left the room, and came back with Charley Bates. Sikes

sat opposite the door, so that the moment the boy entered the room, he saw Sikes's figure.

"Toby," said the boy, falling back, as Sikes turned his eyes towards him, "why didn't you tell me this downstairs?"

There had been something so tremendous in the shrinking off of the three, that the wretched man was willing to appease even this lad. Accordingly, he nodded, and made as though he would shake hands with Bates.

"Let me go into some other room," said the boy, falling still farther back.

"Charley!" said Sikes, stepping forward, "don't you—don't you know me?"

"Don't come nearer me," answered the boy, still retreating, and looking, with horror in his eyes, upon the murderer's face. "You monster!"

Sikes stopped half-way, and they looked at each other; but the murderer's eyes sank gradually to the ground.

"Witness, you three," cried the boy, shaking his clenched fist, and becoming more and more excited as he spoke; "witness, you three—I'm not afraid of him.—If they come here after him, I'll give him up.—I will. I tell you out at once. He may kill me for it, if he likes, or if he dares; but if I'm here, I'll give him up. I'd give him up, if he was to be boiled alive. Murder!—Help! If there's the pluck of a man among you three, you'll help me. Murder!—Help! Down with him!"

Pouring out these cries, the boy actually threw himself, single-handed, upon the strong man, and, in the suddenness of Sikes's surprise, brought him heavily to the ground.

The three lookers-on seemed quite stupefied. They did not interfere; and the boy and man rolled on the ground together.

The contest, however, was too unequal to last long. Sikes had him down, and his knee was on Charley's throat, when Crackit pulled him back with a look of alarm, and pointed to the window.

There were lights gleaming below; the tramp of hurried footsteps crossing the nearest wooden bridge. The gleam of lights increased. The footsteps came more thickly and noisily on.

Then came a loud knocking at the door, and then a hoarse murmur from such a multitude of angry voices as would have made the boldest quail.

"Help!" shrieked the boy, in a voice that rent the air. "He's here! Break down the door!"

"In the King's name," cried the voices without. And the hoarse cry rose again, but louder.

"Break down the door!" screamed the boy.

And strokes thick and heavy rattled upon it, and on the lower window shutters; while a loud huzza burst from the crowd.

"Open the door of some place where I can lock up this screaming boy!" cried Sikes fiercely, running to and fro, and dragging the boy now as easily as if he were an empty sack. "That door—quick!" He flung him in, bolted the door. and turned the key. "Is the downstairs door fast?"

"Double locked and chained," replied Crackit, who, with the other two men, still remained helpless and bewildered.

"The panels—are they strong?"

"Lined with sheet iron."

"And the windows too?"

"Yes, the windows."

"Curse you!" cried the desperate ruffian, throwing up the sash and threatening the crowd. "Do your worst! I'll cheat you yet."

Of all the terrific yells that ever fell on mortal ears, none could exceed the cry of the infuriated throng. Some among the boldest attempted to climb the water-spout and crevices in the wall, and all joined from time to time in one loud, furious roar.

"The tide," cried the murderer, as he staggered back into the room, "the tide was in as I came up. Give me a rope—a long rope. They're all in front. I can drop into Folly Ditch, and clear off by that way. Give me a rope, or I shall do three more murders and kill myself."

The panic-stricken men pointed to where such articles were kept. And the murderer, hastily selecting the longest and stoutest cord, hurried up to the housetop.

All the windows at the back of the house had been long since bricked up, except one small trap in the room where Charley Bates was locked, and that was too small even for the passage of his body. But from this the boy never ceased to call on those without to guard the back; and thus when the murderer appeared at last on the housetop, by the door in the roof, those in front immediately began to pour round, pressing upon each other in an unbroken stream.

The tide was out, and his hope was to let himself down in the ditch, and creep away in the darkness and confusion. He set his foot against the stack of chimneys; fastened one end of the rope tightly and firmly round it, and with the other made a strong running noose, by the aid of his hands and teeth, almost in a second.

This he intended to slip under his armpits, and had just put the loop over his head for that purpose, when, with a yell of terror, he lost his balance, and tumbled over the parapet. The noose was on his neck. It ran up with his weight. There was a

sudden jerk, a terrific convulsion of the limbs;—Sikes had hanged himself!

The murderer swung lifeless against the wall. And Charley Bates, thrusting aside the dangling body, called to the people to come and take him out.

Chapter Sixteen
Fagin's Last Night

Noah Claypole, to save himself, immediately turned informer, and being able to prove that Fagin was "an accessory before the fact"—which means that he had given countenance to Sikes's crime—Fagin was sentenced to be hanged.

He was searched, and then they led him to one of the condemned cells, and left him—alone.

He sat down on a stone bench opposite the door, which served for seat and bedstead; and casting his bloodshot eyes upon the ground, tried to collect his thoughts.

It was very dark. Why didn't they bring a light?

"Light! Light!" and he beat upon the door.

Two men appeared; one bearing a candle, which he thrust into an iron candlestick fixed against the wall.

Rabbis came next day to pray beside him; but he drove them off with curses.

Now he had only one more night to live. And as he thought of this, he cowered down upon his stone bed and thought of the past.

By-and-by Mr. Brownlow and Oliver appeared at the prison, and presented an Order of Admission to the prisoner, signed by one of the sheriffs.

"Is the young gentleman to come too, sir?" said the man whose duty it was to conduct them. "It's not a sight for children, sir."

"It is not, indeed, my friend," rejoined Mr. Brownlow; "but my business with this man is connected with this child."

At that, the man touched his hat, and led them on, through dark and winding ways, towards the cells.

"Fagin!" said the jailer.

"That's me!" cried the prisoner. And he thought he was speaking to the judge. "An old man, my lord—a very old, old man." It had been his answer when the judge had asked him if he had anything to say.

"Here's somebody wants to see you," cried the jailer.

At that, the old man caught sight of Oliver and Mr. Brownlow. And, shrinking to the furthest corner of his seat, he demanded to know what they wanted there.

"You have some papers," said Mr. Brownlow, advancing, "some papers which were placed in your hands, for better security, by a man called Monks."

"It's all a lie," muttered Fagin. "I haven't one—not one."

"For the love of God," said Mr. Brownlow solemnly, "do not say that now, upon the very verge of death; but tell me where they are. You know that Sikes is dead—that Monks has confessed; that there is no hope of further gain. Where are those papers?"

"Oliver," cried Fagin, beckoning to him. "Here, here! Let me whisper to you."

"I am not afraid," said Oliver in a low voice, as he let go the jailer's hand.

"The papers," said Fagin, drawing Oliver towards him, "are in a canvas bag, in a hole a little way up the chimney in the top

of the front room. I want to talk to you, my dear. I want to talk to you."

"Yes, yes," returned Oliver. "Let me say a prayer. Say only one upon your knees, and we will talk till morning."

"Outside, outside," replied Fagin, pushing the boy before him towards the door. "Say I've gone to sleep—they'll believe *you*. You can get me out, if you lead me so. Now then, now then!"

"Oh! God forgive this wretched man!" cried Oliver, with a burst of tears.

"That's right, that's right," said Fagin. "That'll help us on. This door first. Now—now—now!"

"Have you nothing else to ask him, sir?" asked the turnkey.

"Nothing," said Mr. Brownlow.

The door of the cell opened, and the attendants appeared.

"Press on, press on," muttered Fagin. "Faster, faster!"

The men laid hands upon him, and, taking Oliver from his grasp, held Fagin back.

He struggled for an instant, and then sent up a cry that rang in their ears until they reached the open yard.

Next morning he was hanged.

Charley Bates, appalled at Nancy's murder, came to the conclusion that an honest life was best, and struggled hard to lead a better life. After a good deal of suffering, he succeeded at last in getting honest work in the country.

Monks went to America with the portion his father had left him, but he soon squandered it, and, being taken in an act of knavery, he was sent to prison, where he died.

In prison, too, across the seas, died also the Artful Dodger.

Rose married Harry Maylie; and Mrs. Maylie took up her abode with them.

The good doctor missed his friends so much at Chertsey, that he gave up his practice, and came to live near them.

Close, too, lives Mr. Brownlow, with Mrs. Bedwin for his house-keeper, and Oliver for his adopted son.

The suspicious old gentleman often comes to visit them, and Mr. Brownlow loves to joke him on his prophecy concerning Oliver, and reminds him of the night they sat with the watch between them, waiting for his return. Mr. Grimwig always re-torts that, at any rate, he was right that night, and Oliver did not come back; which only makes Mr. Brownlow laugh so heart-ily, that Mr. Grimwig is constrained to laugh as well.

Mr. Brownlow teaches his adopted son, and every day gets more attached to him; for Oliver, tried by adversity, remembers its lessons, in love and mercy to others; giving fervent thanks to God who has protected and preserved him, and brought him safe through all.